THE DETECTIVE GAME

ADAM J. WRIGHT

Copyright © 2024 by Adam J. Wright

All rights reserved.

No part of this book may be reproduced in any form or by any electronic or mechanical means, including information storage and retrieval systems, without written permission from the author, except for the use of brief quotations in a book review.

The locations used in this book are real. Some details may have been changed for fictional purposes.

From initial idea to publication, this book was created entirely by human imagination and hard work.

ALSO BY ADAM J. WRIGHT

THE MURDER FORCE SERIES

EYES OF THE WICKED

SILENCE OF THE BONES

REMAINS OF THE NIGHT

HOUSE OF THE DEAD

DARK PEAK DETECTIVES SERIES

THE DETECTIVE GAME

BURY THE MAIDEN

STANDALONE NOVELS

DARK PEAK

THE RED RIBBON GIRLS

To Miss Mouse

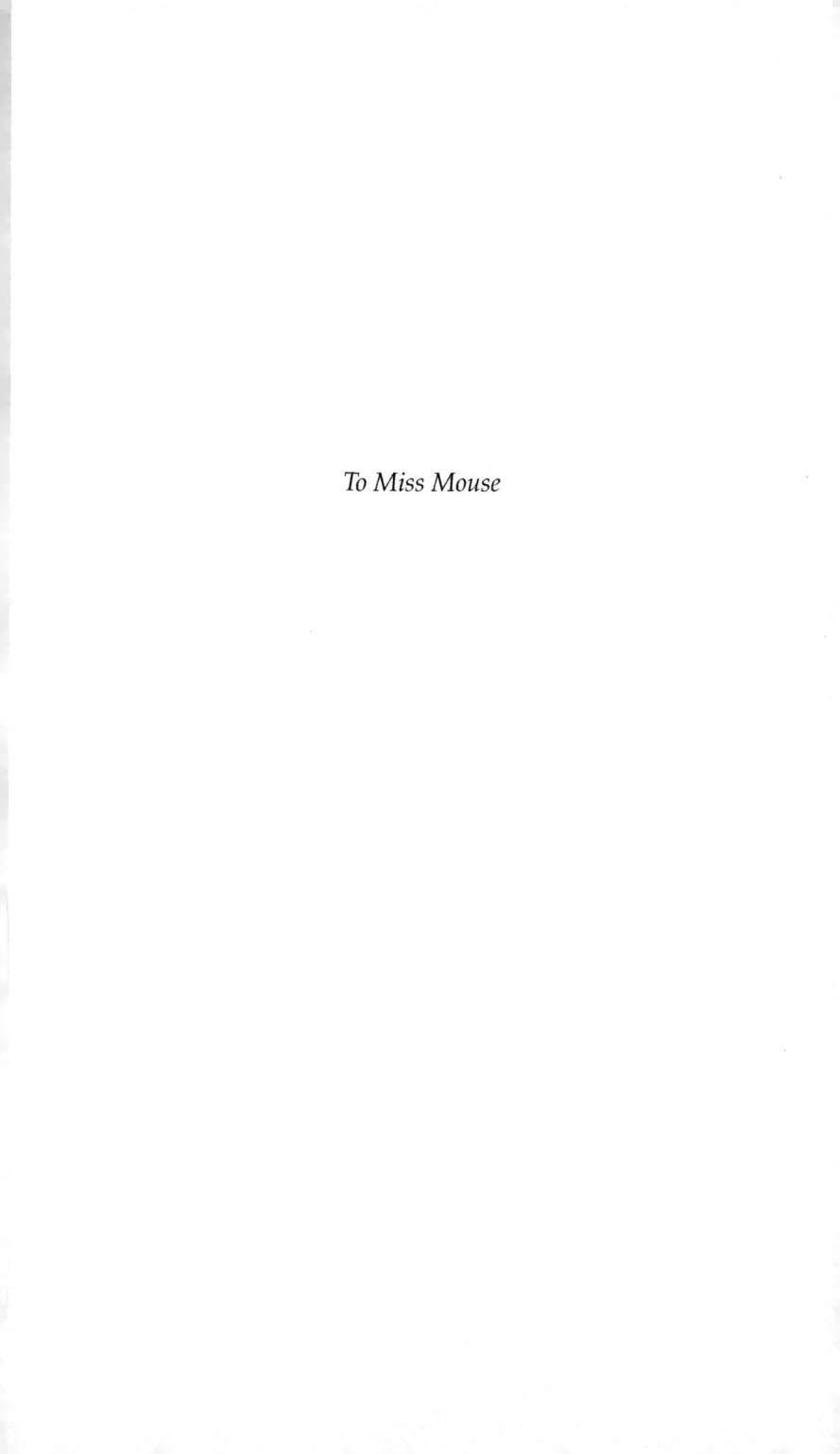

SUNDAY

CHAPTER ONE

"CAN I take my bike over to Michael's house?"

Peggy Jones looked up from the book she was reading —a historical saga about a family fighting to survive the American Civil War— and said, "All right, but I want you back by five. We're having spaghetti for tea."

Sam nodded in agreement —spaghetti was his favourite meal— and sprinted down the garden path to get his bike from the shed.

Peggy, who was reclining on a garden chair in the Sunday afternoon summer warmth, smiled at her son's enthusiasm. She tried to remember if she'd been so full of life at that age.

She supposed she had been, although it was hard to remember being twelve years old. The intervening years' events had mostly overwritten the memories of her younger days.

Sam wheeled his bike to the side gate, then stopped.

"Almost forgot the Mystery File." He leaned the bike against the fence and ran into the house to fetch the notebook which he and his friend Michael had dubbed the "Mystery File."

Peggy had no idea what was in the notebook, or why it was so important to the boys, but she was glad her son had interests that stretched beyond computer games and social media.

He had always been an avid reader and the first books he'd ever read were about solving mysteries: The Secret Seven, The Famous Five, Sherlock Holmes, The Three Investigators, and The Hardy Boys.

Peggy had thought the books old-fashioned, but Sam loved them so much that he had proclaimed, at the age of nine, that he was going to become the world's greatest detective.

His friend Michael seemed to be of the same mind, and this summer the two of them had invented some sort of game that involved the black notebook.

"Are you ever going to tell me what's in the Mystery File?" Peggy asked when Sam reappeared, notebook in hand.

"I can't do that, Mum."

"Why not?"

"Because then it wouldn't be a mystery." He grinned at her as he slid the notebook into the canvas saddlebag on the bicycle's rear mudguard and fastened the buckles to keep it safe.

The bike had once belonged to Peggy's husband, and Sam had never asked for a newer model. Peggy was sure that riding it made Sam feel closer to his dead father.

She never asked about it, though, because some things didn't need to be analysed, and lost their magic if they were examined too closely.

"Remember, five o' clock," she said.

"I'll remember, Mum," He wheeled his bike through the gate.

Then he was gone.

Peggy went back to her book, basking in the warm sunshine. This was the first week of the Summer Holidays and she'd taken it off work to look after Sam. When she returned to her job at the supermarket next week, her mother —who lived a couple of miles away— would take over parental duties during Peggy's shifts.

It had been like this every summer for the last three years, ever since Peggy's husband, David, had passed.

Sam got on well with his grandma and she spoiled him with sweets and homemade apple pie, but he preferred to be at home, Peggy knew. After the upheaval of the past few years, the boy needed security.

At half past four, she went into the house and prepared spaghetti and bolognese sauce, certain that Sam would be home by five, as he had agreed. He was a good boy and always returned when he said he would.

She was so certain of his punctuality that she dished out two meals —one for Sam and one for herself— and placed them on the kitchen table at five.

But there was no sign of her son.

Frustrated, she picked up her mobile and rang him.

There was no answer.

Aware that the dinner was quickly getting cold, she phoned Claire Roberts, Michael's mother. She and Claire were friendly and often had coffee together at the café in the village. Being mothers of twelve-year-old boys who were in the same class at school meant they had a lot in common.

Claire answered immediately. "Hello?"

"Hi, Claire, it's Peggy. Can you send Sam home for his tea? He must have lost track of time."

Claire replied with an edge of worry in her voice. "They haven't come back yet, Peggy."

"Come back?" Peggy felt herself frowning. "From where?"

"They went off on their bikes a couple of hours ago. I told Michael I'd ring him when it was time to come home." She paused. "I rang half an hour ago, but he didn't answer."

A knot of worry tightened in Peggy's stomach. She told herself that boys would be boys and Sam and Michael were probably cycling along one of the footpaths by the hills, where there wasn't a phone signal. Once they realised the time, they'd come straight home.

Wouldn't they?

Despite telling herself not to worry, she said, "I'm going to look for them. Do you know where they went?"

"No, I've got no idea. I'd come with you, but I've got Ellie to think about."

Peggy understood. Claire's daughter Ellie was only

eight months old. Claire could hardly drop everything and go searching for the boys.

"All right. Ring me if they turn up, and I'll do the same if I find them." She sounded much calmer than she felt.

Grabbing her car keys, she rushed out of the house, leaving the two meals on the table to go cold.

An hour and a half later, Peggy had driven along every street in Relby at least three times and travelled further afield to the trails and footpaths that meandered through the untamed landscape that surrounded the village.

She was at her wit's end; the boys could have taken any of the many hiking trails and might be lost in the woods. She refused to acknowledge the most obvious danger; the river that marked the village boundary and ran between the high hills.

Claire had contacted her an hour ago to say that her husband John had returned home from work and was going out to look for the boys. Peggy hadn't heard anything since, neither from Claire nor her husband.

She was going to have to get the police involved, that was all there was to it. She had resisted the idea when it first came to her because contacting the police somehow made everything more serious. But how much more serious could it get? Her son was missing.

A new police station was due to open in the village tomorrow. The building —an old stone house near the pub— had been modernised to be fit for purpose and a police team was supposed to show up in the morning. At least, that's what Peggy had heard. She hadn't taken much notice at the time because she'd believed a police station was the last thing the quiet village of Relby needed.

She couldn't have been more wrong.

She drove to the station. It didn't open until tomorrow, but perhaps someone would be there who could help her.

Passing the Mermaid pub, she saw the stone building with a vintage blue lantern hanging outside, the word POLICE painted in black on the blue glass. At least the refurbishment was in-keeping with Relby's old-fashioned aesthetic.

Her heart dropped when she saw that the interior of the building was cloaked in darkness. There didn't seem to be anyone there at all.

Parking the car, she got out and went to the door anyway, knocking as loudly as she could.

Some of the Mermaid's patrons, sitting outside in the dying sun with their drinks, cast a glance in her direction. Someone shouted, "They're closed until tomorrow, love."

Peggy was going to have to call 999. She had felt — foolishly, perhaps— that talking to someone at the local station wasn't as drastic as calling the police emergency number. It would have made her situation seem less dire than it actually was.

But she was only fooling herself. Sam was missing, and so was Michael. Anything could have happened to them.

"You all right, love?"

The voice made Peggy turn around. A middle-aged woman had come over from the pub, a look of concern on her face. Peggy didn't recognise her; the woman was probably a tourist. A lot of people came here, especially in summer, to hike around the countryside and take in the spectacular views.

"I need the police," Peggy said. She was about to add, "My son is missing," but stopped herself. She wasn't about to vocalise her predicament to a complete stranger. If the woman offered any kind of sympathy, Peggy knew she would break down in tears, unable to stop the flood of emotion. She couldn't allow herself to do that; she had to be strong, for Sam.

She made her way back to the car and dialled 999. When she got through to the police and heard a voice on the other end of the line say, "Police Emergency," the emotions she'd been trying to hold back finally burst through and shattered her resolve.

Hot tears began to flow down her cheeks, and she cried out, "I need help!"

CHAPTER
TWO

DETECTIVE INSPECTOR TOM BRAND sat on a plastic lawn chair on his father's patio, drinking iced lemonade from a tall glass. He'd spent the past hour unpacking his things, which had arrived from London that afternoon.

His feelings about being back in Derbyshire, where he'd grown up but had escaped to work in London, were mixed. On one hand, it was nice to see his father again. On the other, Tom was sure he was going die of boredom before too long.

He had made the move from London because his dad needed help around the house and in the vegetable plots that covered the fields at the back of the house.

Arthritis had dug its claws deep into the old man. Max Brand was struggling. Tom had agreed to transfer from London and get a job nearby, so he could help out when needed.

His old force, the Metropolitan Police, had told Tom

he could return to his old job any time he wanted. He'd been a good detective —great, in fact— and they were sorry to lose him. That was an offer he intended to take them up on as soon as he could. He would persuade his father to move down to the city, where the medical care he could receive for his ailments was far better than anything he could get out here in the sticks.

"So, how does it feel being back here?" his dad asked. He was lying on a sun lounger next to Tom's, glass of lemonade in hand.

"It might take some getting used to," Tom said.

"Once the station opens tomorrow and you get your first case, I'm sure you'll grow to love it here."

"I don't think the cases are going to be beating down the door, Dad," Tom said.

The truth was, he had no idea why the Derbyshire Constabulary had decided to open a police station in Relby at all. There had been some trouble in the area a few years ago regarding several murders, but that was all in the past and hardly warranted a police presence *now*, never mind a dedicated station in the village.

And why assign *him* here? The knowledge and experience he'd gained from London meant he would be a better asset for the force if he was assigned to a bustling city like Derby, not a quiet village like Relby.

He had the feeling he was being sidelined. His new employers didn't know what to do with him, so they'd decided to send him to a brand-new station in the middle of nowhere. A station which could easily be run by a single uniformed constable. It certainly didn't require an on-site detective.

Yet here he was. When tomorrow morning arrived, he would be the local detective for the Relby area.

"You never know," his dad said, "We once had a string of murders around here."

"That was solved," Tom reminded him.

His dad considered that while sipping his lemonade. "Well, I'm sure everyone will still feel safer knowing you're here."

"Thanks." He knew his dad was trying to put a positive spin on the situation, pleased to have his son back home. And it made Tom feel bad that he himself didn't feel so enthusiastic about the situation. But he missed the city already. Being a detective in London meant solving major crimes. What was he going to do here? Look for lost sheep and lock up the occasional drunk?

His mobile buzzed. He fished it out of his pocket and checked the screen. He didn't recognise the number.

"Hello?"

A female voice said, "DI Brand, it's DCI Holt at Ripley Headquarters here. Sorry to bother you on a Sunday evening. I know you don't officially start until tomorrow, but we've had a report of two missing boys in your area. I thought you might like to have a crack at it."

Tom sat up, suddenly alert. "Of course, ma'am. What details do we have?"

"The boys are Sam Jones and Michael Roberts, both twelve years old. Last seen a few hours ago riding from the Roberts' residence on their bicycles. It was Sam's mother who called us." There was a pause while Holt shuffled some papers. "Peggy Jones. She's currently at the Roberts residence with the other mother. I told them someone would be along shortly to take a statement."

"Shouldn't someone be looking for the boys?" Tom said. In missing persons cases, time was of the essence.

"Michael Roberts' father is out there, apparently, and I'm sending a couple of uniforms over there to help. Sam and Michael are probably just having fun somewhere and forgot to come home. You know what young boys are like. They'll probably arrive at the Roberts house before you do." She gave Tom the address and hung up.

Tom slid the phone into his pocket as he got out of the chair.

"Trouble?" his dad asked.

"A couple of missing boys. I'll be back later. Is there anything you need before I go?"

"Tom, my joints might not be what they used to be but I'm not totally useless. You go and find those boys. I'll be fine."

Tom went inside and quickly changed into trousers and a shirt. He grabbed a thick, dark blue jumper as well, in case he was going to be out late, and went downstairs to the kitchen, where his car keys sat on the kitchen counter.

Snatching them up, he went out to the front of the house and got into his black Saab.

He entered the address Holt had given him into the navigation system and set off, hoping the DCI had been right and the boys would turn up before he arrived at the Roberts house.

As he drove, he glanced at the landscape stretching into the distance. There was a lot of wild country out there; too many places where the boys could get hurt or lost.

The hills were dangerous, with rocky crags and steep inclines. The woods that covered much of the area could confuse the unwary, the densely packed trees and undergrowth becoming a maze, seemingly without an exit. The river that snaked through the area was deep and fast-flowing and would probably drag any but the strongest swimmer into its murky depths.

Night would be closing in soon, and Tom hated to think of Sam and Michael out there in that vast expanse of untamed wilderness when darkness fell.

When he arrived at the Roberts house, the front door opened before he'd turned off his engine, and a fair-haired woman rushed down the path towards him.

"Are you the police?"

"Detective Inspector Brand," he told her as he got out of the car.

"I'm Claire Roberts, Michael's mum. Peggy is inside. She's the one who called you. I thought she was overreacting at the time. I was sure the boys would turn up.

But there's still no sign of them." The worry she felt was evident in her voice.

Tom followed her into the house. A woman with dark hair scraped back into a ponytail sat at the kitchen table. Her eyes were red-rimmed, her cheeks blotchy.

"The police are here, Peggy," Claire said.

Peggy looked up and nodded but her expression was devoid of emotion.

"Detective Inspector Brand," Tom said, taking a seat at the table. "You can call me Tom. Police officers are on their way to conduct a search for your boys. Is there any place you think they should start? Somewhere the boys are more likely to have gone?"

"We've checked all their regular haunts," Claire said. "My husband is out there now, looking for them."

Tom nodded, understanding. "I have to ask the next question, I'm afraid. Is there any reason Sam and Michael might have run away?"

"No," Peggy said, her voice barely more than a whisper. "No reason at all."

"And you were the last one to see them." Tom directed his attention to Claire. "How did they seem when they left here? Were they worried or upset about anything?"

Claire shook her head. "Just the opposite. It's the start of the Summer Holidays; they haven't got a care in the world."

"Do they go off on their bikes often?"

"Most days."

"So, nothing seemed unusual."

"No, I told you, everything seemed normal. It was just like any other day. I'm not sure where they are every minute of every day, but they've got their phones with them, and they know to ring me or Peggy if they get into any trouble."

Tom pursed his lips. It sounded like the boys were given free rein to ride their bikes anywhere they wanted. That meant there was no definite starting place for a search. "I'm going to need their phone numbers and a recent picture of them both."

Claire left the room and came back with a framed photo of Sam and Michael. The boys were standing by a riverbank, their bicycles leaning against a tree behind them.

Sam was dark-haired like his mother, while Michael was fair like his. The two friends were grinning at the camera. Sam held a black notebook out in front of him, and Michael was pointing at it making the object the centrepiece of the picture.

"Those are the exact clothes they're wearing now," Claire said, pointing at Michael's jeans and olive-green T-shirt and Sam's shorts and blue T-shirt that bore the word *Sherlock* in white script across the front.

"What's the significance of the notebook?" Tom asked.

Claire sighed. "I wish I could tell you. That's their so-called Mystery File."

"Mystery File?"

"It's part of a game," Peggy said. "They think

they're detectives and that's where they write their clues, or something like that."

"It seems important to them in this picture."

"Oh, it's very important," Claire said. "To them, anyway. They took this picture themselves and insisted I print out two copies, one for each of them."

"Sam keeps his in his bedroom," Peggy said. "He told me that one day they're going to solve a mystery and become famous."

"Do you mind if I remove this from the frame and take it with me?" Tom asked Claire.

She shrugged. "Of course not, as long as I get it back."

"I'll make sure of it." Tom removed the photo from the frame and stood up. "I think I have enough to go on, for now."

The fact was, he didn't have much at all, but he knew there was nothing else to be gained here, no nugget of information that would help him during his search for the boys.

"If they turn up, give me a call," he said, reaching into his pocket for a business card that was not there. His new cards hadn't been printed yet, or if they had, they were at the station in Relby.

He told Claire his phone number, which she wrote on a notepad and set aside.

As he left the house, he wanted to give them words of encouragement, something like, "Don't worry, we'll find them," but he knew he couldn't do that. He wasn't one for false promises, and the way things looked right now, if Sam and Michael didn't arrive home soon, something was very wrong.

So he said nothing as he left the Roberts house and got into his car.

The uniformed officers Holt had sent over would be at the station, so that was Tom's next port of call. He had to familiarise the officers with the case and organise a search.

Before he set off, he had to turn on his headlights.

Night was closing in.

CHAPTER
THREE

WHEN TOM GOT to the station in Relby, the other officers hadn't arrived yet. He parked in the small car park behind the building and used his key to let himself into the stone building that would serve as his place of employment for the foreseeable future.

In contrast to its outward appearance —stone walls, sash windows, and the old-fashioned blue police lantern— the interior of Relby Police Station was thoroughly modern.

Tom flicked on the lights and blinked against the sudden brightness.

A curved front desk had been built in the waiting area, which was furnished with plastic chairs, a low table loaded with magazines, and a box of toys for children.

Tom used a second key to open the door that led to an area for the staff, which consisted of desks, computers, and filing cabinets. Beyond this area, another door bore a plaque which read *DI Tom Brand* and led to his office.

He entered the office and switched on the computer, planning to scan the photograph of Sam Jones and Michael Roberts and print out copies for the officers.

While he waited for the machine to boot up, he sat in the high-backed chair at the desk, trying it out for the first time. He shifted his weight and adjusted the height of the seat, but the chair didn't feel comfortable. Perhaps he'd get used to it over time.

He was about to get up again when his mobile rang. He answered it immediately, hoping it was Claire Roberts ringing to tell him the boys had arrived home safely.

It was DCI Holt. Her tone was flat. "We've had a 999 call from a dog walker on the riverbank. He's spotted something in the river that looks like a body."

Tom felt all the air in his lungs leave his body in a single, heavy sigh.

The DCI continued. "Apparently, he's on a trail that winds around a hill called Stone Peak. Near a bridge. Do you know the place?"

Tom searched his memory. As a child, he'd walked the Stone Peak trail with his parents a number of times. He'd even been to the top of Stone Peak once, with a group of friends. He recalled the narrow bridge that spanned the river. It wasn't too far from the road, if he remembered correctly,

"I know it, ma'am."

"Right, well, get yourself down there and see what's

what." Then she added in a low murmur, "It's always the bloody dog walkers who find the bodies."

"We don't know it *is* a body yet, ma'am."

It was Holt's turn to sigh. "No, I suppose not." She didn't sound convinced.

Tom ended the call and walked back through the empty station, turning off the lights and leaving the photo of Sam and Michael on his desk.

When he was outside and locking up, a police car pulled up next to him and two uniformed officers —one male, one female— got out.

"PC Smith, sir," the male officer said. "And this is my colleague PC Banks. We're here to help you find the two missing boys."

"We've had an emergency call from a member of the public," Tom told them. "We need to go down to the river. Follow me."

The uniforms got back into their car and Tom went to fetch his own. When he left the car park and set off toward the Stone Peak Trail, the other car fell in behind him and stayed close.

It took less than ten minutes to get to the trailhead. A small parking area that consisted of nothing more than a circle of hard-packed dirt was occupied by a silver SUV that Tom assumed belonged to the dog walker. He noted the registration anyway and put his jumper on as he got out of the car. A sudden chill was making itself known in the night air.

Tom took his hiking boots out of the back of the car.

They were brand new; he was sure this wasn't going to be a comfortable walk as he broke them in.

"Do you have boots?" He asked the police constables as they exited their vehicle.

"Yes, sir," PC Banks said.

When everyone was suitably attired, they entered the Stone Peak Trail, which led from the parking area and ran between the river and Stone Peak. The hill towered above the three police officers as they trod carefully along the dark path. Tom and PC Banks held high-powered torches, illuminating the way ahead.

The bridge soon came into view; a dark shape that reached across the river. Tom saw a small flashlight beam on the trail in front of them. The dog walker, he assumed.

"Did you call the police?" he said as he made out a dark shape standing at the river's edge.

The man —Tom could see now that it was a grey-haired man in his sixties, holding a lead to which was attached a fluffy Pomeranian— nodded grimly. "Aye, that was me. I think you'd best have a look at this." He pointed at an area of thick reeds in the water.

Tom swung his torch in that direction but couldn't see what the man was pointing at. He needed to get closer.

Gingerly stepping closer to the water's edge, he aimed the beam of light into the reeds and felt his heart sink. Tangled in the plant stems, just below the surface of the water, was the unmistakeable shape of a child's body. It was suspended there, facedown, arms outstretched, as if gliding beneath the water; held aloft by the river's strong current but also held in place by the thick reeds.

The body wore shorts and a blue T-shirt that undulated in the current. This was Sam Jones.

He turned to PC Smith and said, "We need to tape off this area."

Smith nodded. "I've got crime scene tape in the car."

"Get it. And we need the SOCOs down here, as well as an Underwater Recovery Team."

"On it, Sir."

"And take Mr…" Tom looked at the dog walker expectantly.

"Lewis," the man said. "Charlie Lewis."

"Take Mr Lewis back to the car with you and get a statement."

"Yes, sir." Smith led the dog walker back along the path toward the parking area.

Tom played the torch beam over the river and along the reeds. There was no sign of Michael Roberts.

"What would like me to do, sir?" PC Banks asked.

"Stay here with the body until the SOCOs get here. I'm going to have a look further along the path."

"Yes, sir." The constable took up a position near the edge of the river, standing sentry, hands clasped behind her back.

Tom proceeded along the path, casting his torch beam over the water and into tangles of reeds.

It was fully dark now. Stars appeared in the sky like

bright pinheads and a pale moon cast a silver hue over the rocky crags of Stone Peak.

He had not expected to find a dead boy tonight. His thoughts went to Peggy Jones, sitting at her friend's kitchen table, unaware that her son was gone forever. He had to tell her as soon as he could.

And what was he going to tell Claire Roberts? He wanted to find Michael alive, somewhere on this trail, but his expectations had shifted now, and he anticipated the worst.

The path ahead became muddy. As the torch beam played over the ground, it picked up patterns in the mud. Tom squinted at the illuminated area of ground. There were signs of disturbance here. Footprints and long, thin marks that suggested bicycle wheel tracks. Tom edged closer, careful to not get too close and disturb the scene.

"It looks like the bikes were lying on the ground in this spot," he muttered to himself. The indentations appeared to have been made by the handlebars, and he could see where the bicycles' spokes were pressed into the mud.

So where were the bikes now? In the river? He shone his light at the water but could see nothing.

He hastily took photos of the muddy area with his phone. By the time this place was cordoned off and the SOCOs got here, the marks might have vanished.

Taking a deep breath, he shouted, "Michael, are you out here?"

There was no reply other than the sound of a

panicked group of ducks taking flight somewhere in the darkness.

Was this where Sam had gone into the water? Had the current taken him downstream until he had become caught in the reeds?

He moved farther along the path, searching the ground and the river for any clues that might tell him what had happened here.

Tom mentally went over what he knew. At some point, the bikes had been lying at the edge of the river, in the mud, but now they were nowhere to be found. Sam's body was in the water. Perhaps he had ventured into the river for some reason and had been dragged off his feet by the current.

But where was Michael? He wouldn't simply vanish, along with both bicycles.

Tom shouted for the boy again but got no reply. Even the ducks remained silent.

He walked along the path for what seemed like another mile before it became clear that his search for Michael was fruitless. If the boy was out here, he was ignoring Tom's calls. The darkness hindered a proper search. He might walk right past the boy and not even know he was there. Better to return with a search team in the morning.

He retraced his steps along the trail. At this early stage, it was impossible to piece together exactly what had happened to Sam and Michael. The missing bikes indicated foul play but the fact that Michael was missing as well could mean he had the bikes with him, wherever he was.

The only certainty right now was the fate of poor Sam Jones.

The place where Sam's body had been discovered was lit by powerful lamps which had been set up on the riverbank, and an inflatable dinghy, crewed by two men from the Underwater Recovery Team, floated on the water. A team of divers, wielding bright waterproof torches, explored the reeds, slowly moving downstream.

Sam's body had been recovered from the water and placed on a stretcher, which two men from the Pathologist's Office carried toward the parking area, where brightly lit vehicles awaited their grim cargo.

A tall, gaunt man in a white Tyvek suit waved to Tom and approached him. He was in his fifties, Tom guessed, and his bearing held an air of authority.

"John Yorrick, Crime Scene Investigation," the man said as he got closer. "You must be Inspector Brand. Sorry, I can't shake your hand, these gloves have to go into the evidence bag."

"No problem," Tom said. "Have you found anything of interest? Apart from the body, I mean."

"Not yet. I'd say the boy entered the river elsewhere and the current brought him here. The divers are looking for the other lad, but the river is fast flowing, so he could be much further downstream by now."

"If he's even in the water," Tom said.

"We're assuming he is. Makes the divers scrutinise everything a little bit closer."

"There's an area along the trail that needs to be cordoned off and examined. There are marks in the mud."

Yorrick lowered his chin momentarily, a slight nod "Right, I'll get a team over there."

Tom found Banks standing by one of the portable high-powered lamps and took her with him to the parking area, where PC Smith was leaning on his patrol car. When the constable saw the inspector, he straightened up immediately. "Scenes of Crime and Underwater Recovery Team as requested, sir. And I took a statement from Mr Lewis."

"Good. You two might as well go home and get some rest. We'll resume the search in the morning. Unless..." He turned his attention to the dive team momentarily, leaving the rest unspoken.

"Of course, sir," Banks said, understanding his meaning immediately.

The constables got into their vehicle. Tom did the same, manoeuvring the Saab around the newly arrived Constabulary vehicles to get to the road.

He headed in the direction of the Roberts residence, gritting his teeth as he reflected on his next task.

He had to tell Peggy Jones that her son was dead.

MONDAY

CHAPTER
FOUR

AN INCESSANT BUZZING woke Detective Sergeant Kate Ryan from a dream in which she'd been talking to her mother in a field of brightly coloured wildflowers.

As the sensations of the real world overtook those of the dream, Kate realised her cheeks were damp with tears. Her mother had been dead for twenty-five years. Kate had been six when she'd passed and had no memories of her at all.

Yet she dreamed of her every night.

She reached for the phone on the bedside table, groaning when she saw the time on the bedside clock. Who the hell was ringing at four in the morning?

The name on the screen answered her question. *DCI Holt*. Her boss.

"Hello, ma'am." Her voice sounded croaky. She cleared her throat and sat up.

"Ryan, sorry to wake you." On the other end of the

line, the DCI sounded alert and fully awake. "I've got an assignment for you. I want you to report to Relby in the morning. The new police station."

Kate frowned, confused. "Relby, ma'am?" She'd been working in the area around Matlock, and was part of an ongoing case there, so why did Holt want to send her to Relby? It was in the middle of nowhere.

"Two boys have gone missing," the DCI said. "Well, only one of them is missing now. The other was found in the river."

"Drowned?" She immediately chastised herself for asking such a stupid question. Of course the boy had drowned if he'd been found in the river.

"Looks like it. But there might be more to it than two boys playing near the water and getting into trouble. Their bicycles are missing, according to DI Brand."

She wasn't familiar with the name. "If there's already a DI on the case, ma'am, what do you want me to do?"

"Assist in the investigation. Brand is new, and he's from the Met. They do things differently down there. I want someone with local knowledge on the case. Brand is from the area originally, but he's been away for too long."

"All right, ma'am."

"Good. Be at the station early. We need to show the local community we're doing something about this terrible incident."

"Of course."

"Oh, and Ryan…" She left a silence after her words, waiting for Kate to fill it.

"Yes, ma'am?"

"I want you to report directly to me. I want details about the case. Is that understood?"

Kate had to do what her superior asked, but why was Holt asking her to go behind her colleague's back? She was supposed to report to DI Brand, and he was supposed to pass information along to the DCI. There was a chain of command. The thought of breaking it made a hollowness form in the pit her stomach.

"What about my caseload in Matlock? I'm in the middle of an investigation and if I leave now— "

"Someone else will take over your workload," Holt said flatly, making it clear that the new assignment to Relby wasn't a request. It was an order, and Kate wasn't going to be able to get out of it no matter how hard she tried.

Sighing heavily, Kate said, "I'll report to Relby in the morning, ma'am."

"Good. Let's find out what happened to those poor boys and bring some closure to their families and to the community."

"Yes, ma'am." She ended the call. Holt had said all the right things, but her words had rung hollow.

Sitting in the darkness of her bedroom, Kate decided that the only way she was going to get out of the unsavoury assignment would be to solve the case quickly. Then there would be no reason for Holt to keep her in Relby; she'd have to send her back to Matlock.

Getting out of bed —there was no way she was going back to sleep now— she pulled back the curtains and looked out into the early morning gloom. The town looked as if it were asleep, slumbering beneath a pale moon.

Kate turned to the wardrobe and began placing clothes on the bed. She needed to pack a suitcase. Relby was too far for her to commute, and she needed to stay close to the investigation. She'd find a B&B and charge it to expenses.

She collected various toiletries from the bathroom and deposited them on the bed next to the clothes. Her suitcase was in the spare bedroom. She would get it later and try to cram everything inside. The pile on the bed looked as if she were going away for months, but she knew she had to pack for every eventuality. It might be the height of Summer, but in Derbyshire, cold weather could close in at any time, especially on the hills.

Kate had no idea to what kind of terrain the investigation would take her, so she had to be prepared for anything.

An hour later, the suitcase was packed and sitting by the door. Kate brewed herself a much-needed coffee and sat at the kitchen table with her laptop. She searched the local news and found a report about the missing boys immediately.

One Boy Dead, One Missing, the headline of a local news outlet proclaimed. Kate read the article but there was scant information. According to the report, Michael

Roberts and Sam Jones, both aged 12, had gone missing yesterday evening. Sam's body was recovered from the river and Michael was still missing. The article listed the police hotline number and a photo of Michael Roberts' face beneath an appeal for witnesses.

It didn't tell her much. It didn't even mention the bikes. She'd get all the details from DI Brand when she saw him later. The titbits he'd fed to the press amounted to nothing more than the bare facts. She'd have done the same if she were in his position. Put out enough information for the public to be aware of the missing boy and that was that. She'd run afoul of the media once or twice and assumed Brand had also. It was part of being a detective.

She searched the Net for B&Bs near Relby while she finished the coffee and found one that looked perfect. Located in the village itself, which meant it must be close to the police station.

She booked herself in for a week, hoping that would be all the time she'd need.

She knew she'd been chosen for this task not because of her investigative talents, but simply because she was from the Dark Peak area. Her family still lived there, and she visited often. She knew how the small communities and the farms functioned, how the people who lived among the hills and rolling landscape thought. She was used to the wild terrain and the dangers it presented.

The locals would see DI Brand as an outsider. He may have been born among the peaks, but he'd left for the city, which was as good as never having set foot in the Peak District, as far as some of the locals were concerned.

The underlying distrust didn't make for an easy police investigation. Brand might have trouble getting people to open up to him. They might even withhold important information that could help the investigation.

Kate would have no such problems talking to the locals. She was one of them. That was the only reason Holt had chosen her for this assignment; to get the witnesses to open up.

That, and to report directly on the case.

She swallowed the sour taste that thought left in her mouth. If Holt didn't trust Brand, then why had she put the DI in charge of Relby station?

Why had she hired Brand in the first place?

She wasn't going to get any answers sitting here. She had to get to Relby. Perhaps meeting Brand would give her an insight into the situation she'd been unwillingly tossed into.

She dragged her heavy suitcase outside. The sky was cloudless, and the day promised to be warm in a few hours, but last night's chill still hung in the air.

Kate loaded everything into her green Jeep Renegade and set off for Relby while her neighbours slept.

As she drove out of Matlock, the early morning news came on the radio.

The search continues for missing twelve-year-old Michael Roberts, who was last seen with his friend Sam Jones, also twelve, in the Peak District yesterday. Sam's body was later discovered by a dog walker near Stone Peak, but Michael is still missing. Police are appealing for witnesses and have asked anyone with knowledge of Michael's whereabouts to call the incident hotline.

Kate set her gaze firmly on the road ahead. If Michael Roberts was still alive, she would do everything in her power to find him.

CHAPTER FIVE

TOM WOKE UP DISORIENTED, sitting bolt upright in bed. He'd slept fitfully, his mind running over and over last night's events and refusing to slow down.

He slipped out of bed and checked his phone. If there had been any developments, someone would have rung him. He was afraid he might have been so exhausted that he hadn't heard the call.

But there was nothing on the phone. No message to say Michael Roberts had been found.

Tom rubbed his eyes as last night's conversation with Peggy Jones replayed in his head. She had taken the news of her son's death exactly as he had expected. First denial, then horrific realisation, and finally weeping uncontrollably while Claire Roberts tried to comfort her.

As Tom had left the house, Peggy had cried out,

"Find the person who did this." The raw anguish behind the words had made Tom flinch. He'd climbed into his car and had sat there for quite some time, gripping the steering wheel until his knuckles turned white, then releasing the pressure before repeating the action, trying to quell a surge of emotion that rose within him in response to the wailing that came from within the house.

Find the person who did this.

Peggy obviously didn't believe her son had fallen into the river by accident. And Tom was inclined to agree with her. It was still early days, but too much didn't add up. The missing bikes, for one. Sam's missing friend, for another.

Holt was sending uniformed officers over today to take part in a wide-scale search. Tom had spent most of last night —after leaving Peggy and Claire— at the station, poring over a map of the area and working out search patterns.

He'd used the section of riverbank where Sam had been found as a starting point and covered the map with ever-widening circles that indicated areas to be searched.

He went to the window and pulled back the curtains. At least the weather was on his side; there wasn't a cloud in the sky. That meant dry terrain for the search parties to navigate, much easier than thick mud and slippery rocks.

He showered and put on hiking trousers and a dark blue jumper before going downstairs.

His father was in the kitchen, standing before an open cupboard, staring at its contents. The old man looked frail. His shirt and trousers hung loosely from his thin frame as if they were draped over a clothesline.

"You okay, Dad?"

"Of course, of course. Just trying to decide what to make you for breakfast."

"You sit down. I'll make breakfast for both of us."

"Are you sure? You've got a busy day ahead, with the search and all."

"All the more reason to have a hearty breakfast." Tom looked into the open cupboard and took out a box of oats. "How about some porridge?"

"Yes, that would be wonderful." His dad shuffled over to the old pine table that had served as the centrepiece of the kitchen since Tom had been a child, wincing as he sat down

"Tea?" Tom said, filling the kettle.

"Yes, please. The pot's on the counter over there. Here, let me…"

"You stay put. I've got it all under control." Tom opened the lid of the teapot. Dust rimed the inside. He took it over to the sink and washed it out.

"I don't use the pot when it's just me," his father said by way of an explanation.

Tom nodded, understanding. The teapot, with its small lid, was too difficult for his dad's arthritic fingers to manage. He tossed three tea bags into the freshly washed pot and waited for the kettle to boil.

"Do you know what I'd really like?" his dad said.

"What's that?"

"Some toast. I can't work the toaster anymore. Can't press the lever down."

"Leave that to me." Tom placed four slices of bread into the toaster and got them started while he poured the water —which had now boiled— from the kettle into the teapot. He grabbed two mugs and placed them on the table, along with the pot. "I'll pour it out in a minute."

He got the porridge started on the hob and said, "What do you normally have for breakfast?"

"I usually skip it."

"What about lunch?"

"A microwave meal suffices. I can work the microwave fairly easily. Dinner is the same."

No wonder his dad's clothes were falling off him. "Right, I won't be here for lunch, but I'll cook us up a nice dinner tonight. How does pasta sound?"

His father gave him a wide, genuine smile. "Wonderful."

"That's settled, then." The toast popped out of the toaster and Tom took it to the table, placing two of the slices on a small plate in front of his dad. "What would you like on these?"

"I think there's a jar of marmalade in the cupboard. I haven't had marmalade in a while."

Tom found the unopened jar and took it over to the table, popping it open on the way. He found butter in the fridge and placed that in front of his dad as well.

Taking a knife from the cutlery drawer, he said,

"Would you like me to put the butter and marmalade on for you?"

His dad looked sheepish. "Would you? I feel terrible not even being able to spread butter on my toast."

"Don't worry about it, Dad. That's why I'm here."

"And I feel awful about that, Tom. If it wasn't for me, you'd be living happily in London, getting on with your life."

'We're not going over that again," Tom said, scraping butter onto the toast. "I told you before, I want to I help." It was true. He couldn't go about his "happy" life in London knowing his father was struggling. There was no part of his character that would let him ignore a family member in trouble.

His dad nodded. "I know that, but I also know you aren't one for the countryside. It used to amaze your mum and me how much you wanted to move to a city. Most people escape to the *countryside*, you know. How we raised you to be the opposite, I'll never know."

His eyes glistened and he reached out to lay a hand over Tom's arm. "She'd be proud of you, you know."

"Who? Mum?" It was a subject they didn't broach often. "Proud of me because I'm a London detective?" *Was*, he reminded himself. It already felt like a lifetime ago.

"No, not that. Although she was proud of everything you did. I mean because you're here helping me."

Tom smiled and slid the plate of toast towards his dad before leaving the table and moving to the hob. He concentrated on stirring the porridge until it was the correct consistency and then divided it into two bowls.

Returning to the table, he placed one bowl in front of his father and began to eat the other.

They ate in silence for a while until his father said, "I hope you find that poor boy today."

Tom nodded. "So do I." Outside, the weather was warming up, promising a hot Summer's day, but last night had been chilly. If Michael Roberts was still alive, he'd be cold, tired, and hungry.

When he'd finished eating, Tom said goodbye to his father and went out to the car. His dad came outside a few moments later, holding a waterproof jacket. "Before you go, you might need this. They say it's going to rain later."

"Who does?"

"The weather people on the radio."

Tom shrugged. There was no sign of rain as far as he could see, but he tossed the jacket onto the backseat anyway.

He took a moment to glance at the distant hills and woods.

His father looked out over the landscape as well. "That poor boy could be anywhere out there, lost and alone."

His dad was right. Michael could be anywhere in that harsh wilderness. Anywhere at all.

He arrived at the Relby station to find the building surrounded by a media circus. Mobile broadcast vans lined the narrow street. Miles of cable snaked from the vans to camera crews, sound crews, and hordes of journalists with microphones.

Tom parked behind the building, in between two police vans, and marched to the front door of the station, only to find it locked. As he took out his key, he heard someone say, "That's the detective in charge of the case."

Journalists began running in his direction, microphones held out in front of them as if they were running a relay race and about to pass the baton.

They all threw questions at him at the same time while Tom hurriedly pushed the key into the door.

"Inspector Brand, will the search for Michael continue today?"

"Detective, do you think Michael Roberts is still alive?"

"Inspector, was the death of Sam Jones the result of foul play?"

Tom slid inside the building and locked the door behind him. When he turned away from the door, he realised the lights were on. He jumped when he saw a woman sitting behind the front desk.

She wore her grey hair in a bun and a pair of thick-rimmed glasses perched on her nose, giving her the look of a librarian.

"Sorry to scare you, Inspector," she said, coming

around the desk and holding out her hand. "Hazel Owens. I'll be working the front desk. Well, half the time I will, anyway. Derek and I share shifts. So, it'll either be him or me holding the fort." She indicated the locked door. "Literally, today, it seems."

Tom remembered Holt telling him the front desk would be manned by two people working shifts and that there would be a support team arriving on Wednesday.

"Tom Brand," he said, shaking Hazel's hand. "Is anyone else here?"

"About two dozen uniformed officers," she said, gesturing at the door that led to the inner offices, "They've come to help search for that missing lad. I've put tea and biscuits out for them, so they should be in good spirits."

"Good thinking."

"Would you like a cuppa, Inspector?"

"I'm fine thank you, Hazel." he opened the door and entered the room. The uniformed officers filled the room, most of them standing in small groups, others sitting on desks and perched on windowsills. The low buzz of expectant conversation died down as Tom entered.

He hadn't had the time last night to prepare a speech, but he'd briefed enough teams during his career that it was second nature to him.

"I'm DI Brand," he said, raising his voice enough to be heard at the back of the room. "Today, we're going to be looking for Michael Roberts. We're also looking for two bicycles. These are the bikes Michael and Sam rode to the river at Stone Peak. One of them is quite old, with a distinctive saddlebag on the rear mudguard. Impressions in the riverbank indicated that the bikes had been lying there at some point, but they are now missing. The bikes may contain evidence, so if you find them, treat them as you would any crime scene."

He passed a stack of photocopied pictures of Michael, Sam, and the bicycles to the nearest officer. "Pass those around, please."

Tom stepped into his office and brought out the map he'd marked with search grids. He held it up against the wall. "We'll work in two teams. The first team will start here, on the riverbank at the foot of Stone Peak, and work out from there in all directions."

"Does that include going up the Peak itself, sir?" someone asked.

There was some laughter, but Tom quelled it. "Yes, that includes climbing the Peak. It's steep, but I'm sure that won't be a problem for a bunch of fit police officers like yourselves. However, I do have to remind you to be careful. We don't want to have to call the helicopter to get you off the side of the hill, do we?"

There was some laughter and a few groans of displeasure as the officers realised the scale of the search ahead of them.

"It's not going to be easy," Tom said, "but Michael could have gone up the hill, so we have to go up there as well."

A few officers nodded in agreement.

"I'll lead the first team," Tom said. "That will be Team Alpha. A second team, Team Bravo, will be searching this area of woodland to the north. The main path curves around the base of Stone Peak, but a second path leads to the woods. It's possible that Michael went that way. I need a volunteer to be in charge of the second team."

"I volunteer, sir," said a voice from the back of the room.

Tom looked in that direction and saw a young woman with long brown hair tied back in a ponytail. She wore black trousers and a white blouse. Although she was diminutive in stature, she pushed her way to the front in a calm and assured manner, unintimidated by the big, burly police officers around her.

"And you are?" Tom asked.

"DS Kate Ryan, sir."

Tom was taken aback. Another detective. He was used to working with other detectives in London, but Holt hadn't told him there would be a second detective on this case.

He hid his surprise with a nod. "All right, DS Ryan, you're in charge of Team Bravo."

She nodded back to him.

"Split yourselves into two teams." Tom told the officers, "And get yourselves in the vans. There are a lot of reporters out there and they'll be asking questions. I don't need to remind you to keep quiet. All communication with the media will be done through official channels. That doesn't mean us, it means the higher-ups, so no comment, is that understood?"

The officers murmured in agreement as they left the room. DS Ryan stayed behind.

"By the look on your face, I don't think you were expecting me to be here, sir," she said.

"I wasn't," Tom said. "The DCI didn't mention anything about another detective." That sounded a bit unwelcoming, so he added, "Glad to have you onboard, though. And there's no need to call me sir; guv will do just fine."

"Yes, guv."

"Right, let's get to it," he said, handing her a map. "Hopefully, we can bring Michael Roberts home today."

He left the station, with Ryan following close behind. The press descended on the two detectives like hungry vultures swooping from the sky to tear apart a carcass.

Tom waved them away with a stern, "No comment."

When he was in his car and starting the engine, he wondered why Holt had sent DS Ryan to work on the case.

She must have done something wrong for the DCI to send her all the way out here, to the proverbial Siberia. It wasn't a place anyone would volunteer to work.

Perhaps she wanted to make a name for herself, and working on a case like this, which was becoming more high-profile every minute, was her way of doing that.

Tom didn't really care, as long as she helped find the missing boy.

He followed the police vans out of the car park and out of the village.

In the distance, Stone Peak loomed against the sky like a sleeping giant.

Despite the brightness of the day, rocky crags and twisted trees shrouded the hillside in dark shadows.

CHAPTER SIX

KATE TUCKED her trousers into her hiking boots and waited while the uniformed officers poured out of the vans and arranged themselves into two teams in the parking area.

DI Brand —the guv'nor— was similarly donning a pair of outdoor boots, leaning against the back of his car while he laced them up.

Kate wasn't sure what to make of him yet. Their meeting had been too brief to form an opinion, although he'd spoken to the troops with confidence, which was a point she was willing to put in the "good boss" column of her mental tally sheet.

The journalists had followed them here from the police station but kept their distance, skulking around their vehicles across the road. They couldn't go any farther; the trailhead had been cordoned off with police tape and two officers had been stationed here since last night.

The Underwater Recovery Team was already on the water. A rubber dinghy floated in the middle of the river and divers swam beside it, plunging down to the riverbed and surfacing again like seals searching for fish. But what these divers sought was something much grimmer.

Brand handed out rucksacks containing bottles of water to the officers and then gave one to Kate. He shrugged the final pack onto his own back. "Ready to go?"

She stuffed her lightweight, waterproof jacket into the rucksack and nodded. The weather forecast had predicted clear skies earlier in the day and rain this evening. She knew from experience how changeable the weather could be in this area; sunny and hot one minute and pouring with rain the next was not out of the ordinary.

The trek ahead didn't bother her; she was used to walking the trails and footpaths in this area. She'd been up to the top of Stone Peak multiple times in her younger days.

The DI handed her a walkie talkie. "Phone reception is spotty around here at best. We'll use these to stay in contact."

Kate slid the device into a side pocket of the rucksack and followed him to the trailhead. There was just enough room for two people to walk abreast on the trail, so she and Brand took the lead while the uniforms fell in behind.

As they passed the spot where the dinghy was

anchored in the middle of the river, the DI gave a quick wave to a man in the bow of the craft. The man waved back and shook his head, communicating the fact that the recovery team's efforts had failed to find anything on the riverbed so far.

That was a good thing. Kate wanted this case to be solved as soon as possible but she certainly didn't want Michael to be found in the water. She wanted him to be discovered alive and well. Preferably today. She didn't really mind if Brand's team discovered the boy, but she'd rather Team Bravo take the glory.

Logically, it made more sense to her that Michael was in the woods and not on the Peak. If something had frightened him, he would naturally seek cover. Animal instincts run deep, especially in times of stress or fear. The woods provided shelter and hiding places. The Peak meant exposure to the elements and more chance of being seen.

Seen by whom?

The person who had probably murdered Sam, of course. But who was that? What motive drove someone to murder a twelve-year-old boy?

Those questions remained mysteries at the moment, but Kate was confident the answers were out there somewhere. All she had to do was find them.

But first, she had to find out what the DI knew that hadn't been released to the media.

"Are there any relevant details about this case, guv?" she asked. "Anything we've withheld from the press?"

"To be honest there aren't many details at all," he told her. "The SOCOs have examined the area where the prints were found in the mud and they're analysing the results."

"Prints?" She was hoping he meant fingerprints. That would make everything move along much more quickly.

"Impressions in the ground. It looks like the bikes were lying in the mud right at the edge of the river."

"But they're gone now." She mulled that over. Either Michael had taken the bikes with him when he'd left the area, or someone else had taken them, probably to destroy evidence.

As Brand had mentioned at the station, the bikes were crime scenes and could hold evidence that would shed some light on what had happened to the boys.

"Yes, they're gone now," he said. "Finding those bikes is our top priority after finding Michael."

"Perhaps we'll find Michael *and* the bikes," Kate offered.

The DI pursed his lips. "I doubt it, to be honest. I've been thinking about it, and I can't see any reason why Michael would leave the area and take both bikes with him."

She had to agree. Two bikes would be difficult for a boy of Michael's age to handle, especially over rough terrain.

Brand fell silent. Kate followed suit, taking in the view around her. The sunlight reflecting on the water. The steep rise of Stone Peak. The distant woods to the north. This was the environment she knew and loved, and the beauty of its wild places was why she never wanted to be anywhere else.

She couldn't comprehend why Tom Brand would swap this spacious, natural environment for the crowded city streets of London.

After a few minutes of silent walking, they reached the muddy area Brand had told her about, although the footprints of the Scenes of Crime Officers were more distinct than any markings relating to bicycles.

"Team Alpha, stop here," the DI called to the uniformed officers. "Team Bravo, continue on with DS Ryan." He held up his walkie talkie and said to Kate, "Stay in touch."

She nodded and turned the device on before slipping it into her pocket. Twelve officers followed her, leaving twelve behind with Brand.

Kate picked up the pace, eager to get to the search area. If Michael Roberts was in the woods, her team would find him, she was sure of that.

The trail skirted Stone Peak and then forked; continuing West around the Peak while also branching North to the woods. Kate took the Northern route, and her fellow officers followed.

"What's to say the lad didn't stay on the main path and go around the Peak?" she heard someone mumble to a colleague behind her.

"No one is saying he didn't," she said, turning around and addressing the officers *en masse* because she didn't know who had spoken. "But we have to start somewhere, and the DI has decided we start in the woods. If we don't find anything there, then we explore other options."

"We could split up," someone suggested.

"No, we aren't going to do that. We need a long, shoulder-to-shoulder line of people for a fingertip search of the woods. We can't risk missing anything. If we split up, the line would cover half as much area."

She hoped the DI appreciated her defending him, although, of course, he would never learn of this exchange.

With the dissension in the ranks quieted, Kate led Team Bravo to the edge of the woods and stopped. The trail continued beneath the trees, winding gently like a lazy snake through the dappled shadows.

"All right," Kate said, "everyone spread out. Shoulder-to-shoulder. We're going to walk forwards slowly, checking the ground directly in front of us for anything that could be related to the reason we're here. If you see anything that could be relevant, put your hand up and shout, "Find." Every ten steps, we're going to call Michael's name and tell him we're the police. He might be hiding in here somewhere, afraid to come out. Does everyone understand what to do?"

Nodding and answering in the affirmative, the officers spread out, six on each side of Kate.

"Just remember," she said, trying to lighten the mood, "this is preferable to climbing Stone Peak on a hot day like today."

The team murmured agreement, every eye trained

on the ground in front of them. The atmosphere had shifted. Everyone had a job to do and was eager to do it.

Kate called out Michael's name, waited a few seconds for a response that never came, and then nodded to the team.

They moved as one into the woods.

CHAPTER SEVEN

CLIMBING Stone Peak on a hot day like today hadn't been Tom's best idea ever. After searching the trees at the base of the Peak and coming up empty, he and his team had begun to ascend the incline that led up to the top of the steep hill.

The search was arduous. As well as contending with aching legs and burning lungs, the team had to check every inch of ground in front of them for possible evidence. It was slow-going and tiring.

There were paths that led up the hill; designated routes that took hikers to the top so they could appreciate panoramic views of the Peak District. But not here, not on this part of the hill. Tom and his team had to eschew the traditional routes and clamber over rough terrain scarred with crags and gullies. The higher they climbed, the more the Peak sapped their energy.

Tom looked over his shoulder. The dinghy on the

river looked tiny from up here, the divers ants scurrying around it.

He wiped sweat from his brow and held up a hand to the team. "We'll take a quick break." Sitting heavily on the grass, he tried to slow his breathing as it rasped in his throat. When had he become so unfit? Had city life —where everything was accessible by car or the Tube— stolen so much from him? True, he'd put on a few pounds over the last couple of years, but he hadn't realised just how out of shape he was until now.

He took a bottle of water out of his rucksack and poured some of it into his mouth. It cooled his throat as he swallowed. After a second sip, he dabbed some of the liquid onto his forehead.

Ignoring the ache in his back and legs, he stood up again and replaced the bottle, calling out, "Okay, let's continue," to the team as he swung the rucksack back over his shoulder. Realising he was unfit was one thing; showing that weakness to anyone else was quite another.

They resumed the trudge up the hill, moving at a painstakingly slow pace while checking the ground for anything that might indicate Michael had come this way. Tom wondered how likely it was that the boy had come up here. He'd already concluded it was unlikely, but every possibility had to be checked. He wouldn't be able to live with himself if it later turned out that a clue to Michael's whereabouts had been sitting on the hillside above the crime scene all the time and he hadn't bothered to look for it.

"Find!"

The shout had come from Tom's left. He turned in that direction to see a uniformed officer standing in a deep gully. Only the officer's upper body was visible, the rest obscured by the high sides of the natural trench in which he stood.

Making his way over to the officer, Tom whispered to no one in particular, "Please don't let it be a body."

A chill breeze began to whisper over the hillside.

As Tom reached the deep scar in the ground —the result of water running down the hillside over the years, eroding soil and rock until it formed a miniature ravine— he looked down and breathed a sigh of relief. The find wasn't the body of the lost boy at all; it was a small Tupperware container —no larger than a deck of cards— half-buried in the soil.

Tom stared at it for a moment. That it had been buried here purposefully and hadn't arrived at this spot by accident was certain. The plastic box sat perfectly in the soil with only its lid showing above the dirt. The lid itself was covered with loose soil, making Tom think the box had once been completely buried, but had been revealed by strong winds battering the hillside, or perhaps by water running down the gully.

The question was: who had buried it here? And more importantly: what was in the box? He wasn't about to disturb the soil to look through the transparent lid at the contents. Better to leave everything undisturbed until it could be examined properly.

"Get Forensics up here," he said. "Someone needs to wait here until they arrive."

"I'll do it, sir," said the officer who had made the find.

"Right," Tom said, addressing the rest of the troops. "Let's see if we can find anything else up here."

CHAPTER
EIGHT

IT WAS cool in the woods. A slight breeze rustled the leaves of the trees, making it sound as if they were whispering to each other as the line of police officers carefully searched the undergrowth below.

Kate stood on the snaking trail, carefully checking the hard-packed dirt in front of her as well as the areas where dense undergrowth blurred the edges of the path. Low-lying plants covered the ground, carpeting it with greenery while at the same time reaching out new tendrils to expand their dominion of the woodland floor. Kate knew the names of some of these plants: *Cardamine Impatiens*, recognisable by their fern-like leaves, and Mountain Currant, which draped itself over anything in its way.

Her father had taught her about the flora of the area from a young age. It was something her mother had been interested in, apparently, and he had wanted to pass that knowledge to Kate.

Her mother, Laura, had loved the woods and hills, a fact that brought solace to Kate's father whenever he thought about his wife. She had perished on a hillside while hiking alone, one of her favourite pursuits. Kate's dad always said that at least she had died doing something she loved.

Kate didn't see it that way. She wondered why her mother had gone hiking that day at all. It was New Year's Day, a day to spend with family, as far as Kate was concerned. One of the worst storms in decades had been forecast. As an experienced fell walker, her mother must have known the weather was closing in, must have known the dangers of going out. She had been an expert in wilderness survival techniques, yet her body had been found on an exposed part of a hillside. That didn't make any sense to Kate. An expert survivalist would seek shelter and wait there until the weather conditions were less dangerous.

Both the Mountain Rescue team and the police theorised that Laura Ryan must have become confused by the storm and been unable to find her way to a place of safety.

That explanation had never satisfied Kate, but what did she know? Her mother's death had occurred twenty-five years ago, and Kate had only been six years old at the time.

She brought her focus from the past to the present. She might not have been able to save her mother, but she could still save Michael Roberts.

She called out his name and waited for a response.

But no one replied to her call. The only sounds were of birds and the wind.

Something caught her attention. A flash of white through a gap in the trees to her left. Kate squinted against the dappled sunlight and realised it was a house. The building sat on a low hill beyond the edge of the woods. If someone lived there, they might have seen Michael come this way. If the place was abandoned, Michael could be inside; perhaps hiding or maybe even injured and in need of assistance.

Kate turned to a female constable who was pushing back the *Impatiens* to examine the ground beneath. "I need you to come with me, PC…"

"Dalton." The officer stood. She was tall, towering over Kate and most of the men on the team. "PC Lily Dalton."

Kate addressed the team. "Listen up, everyone. PC Dalton and I are going to investigate that building over there. I want the rest of you to continue the search here."

Kate and the PC trudged through the undergrowth toward the distant house. It was hard going, stepping over fallen branches and wading through a sea of vines and ferns, and when they reached the edge of the woods, a fence barred access to the field beyond. Weathered wooden posts had been driven into the ground, following the tree line, and taut wire ran between them.

Dalton, steadying herself on one of the wooden posts vaulted over the wire easily. Kate, steadying herself on the post in the same manner, stepped onto the top wire and climbed over.

It was clear now that the building on the hill was a farmhouse. The field in which Kate and her colleague now stood was devoid of anything but grass, but the neighbouring field, separated from this one by a bramble hedge, was occupied by a dozen cows. The animals were chewing grass, moving slowly in the summer heat.

"Come on," Kate said, leading Dalton to a metal gate at the far end of the field. She hoped she wasn't going to have to climb that as well.

The gate was secured by a simple metal band that lifted easily from the fence post over which it was looped. Kate and Dalton went through and secured the gate behind them.

A rooster strutted around the yard, eyeing them suspiciously. From a barn on her left, Kate could see eyes peering at her from the darkness. It took her only a few seconds to realise the eyes belonged to a pair of goats.

The farmhouse door opened and a small woman with mousey hair, wearing a knee-length floral dress and an apron covered with flour marks, came out onto the step. "Who are you?"

"Hello," Kate said, smiling to put the woman at ease. The woman seemed nervous, wringing her hands on the edge of the apron, her eyes darting from Kate to PC Dalton and back again. Her fear was understandable considering the fact that Kate and Dalton had just appeared from the field, but surely Dalton's uniform should be reassurance enough that they were here on official business.

"We're from the Constabulary," Kate said. "Detective Ryan and PC Dalton. I was wondering if we could have a quick word with you. Do you live here?"

The woman nodded. She didn't come any further than the step, so Kate moved forward slowly. She was reminded of a time when she was ten years old and had spotted a wild deer in the woods. Her dad had told her to move slowly toward the animal in case she spooked it and sure enough, as soon as Kate had taken two steps forward, the deer had taken flight, bounding through the woods and disappearing in seconds.

The woman on the step looked like she was either going to bolt inside the house and lock all the doors or faint right there in front of them.

She did neither of those things. She simply nodded, continuing to worry the edge of the apron.

"What's your name?" Kate asked.

"Wendy." The woman swallowed. "Wendy Gibbon. You can't be here."

Kate took another step forward. "Why do you say that?"

"I mean, what are you doing here?" Wendy corrected herself. She hesitated for a second and then added, "How can I help you?" A smile appeared on her face, but it didn't reach her eyes. They darted around the yard, as if looking for a place to run and hide.

"I'd just like to ask you some questions," Kate said. "We're looking for a missing boy."

"Missing boy? I don't know anything about any missing boy. You'll have to ask someone else."

"Is there anyone else here we can ask? Do you live alone?"

Wendy shook her head.

As if on cue, a male voice from inside the house called, "Mum, where are you?"

"I'll be there in a minute, Charlie," she shouted.

"Is that your son?" Kate took another step forwards. "Can we speak to him?"

"No, you can't. Now, you'll have to leave. We don't know anything about any missing boy here. "

A heavyset young man dressed in shorts, a blue T-shirt with a white *Fortnite* logo across the chest, and a plain, tan-coloured baseball cap came out onto the step. He was in his early twenties.

"Come on, Mum," he said, tugging at Wendy's apron, ignoring the two strangers in the yard. "The biscuits are going cold."

"We haven't put them in the oven yet, Charlie," she told him. "They can't go cold when they haven't even been warm."

"Charlie," Kate ventured. "Hello, my name is Kate."

He looked at her, narrowing his eyes suspiciously. "Hello."

"Go back inside, Charlie," Wendy said. "I'll be there in a minute."

He huffed, dropping his shoulders and head as he stomped back into the house.

"Mrs Gibbon," Kate said. "I just want to know if you've seen this boy." She took the photo of Michael Roberts from her pocket and held it out to the woman.

Wendy refused to take it. She shook her head. "Never seen him."

"Could I ask your son?"

"He's never seen him either. You really should go now."

"Perhaps if Charlie saw the photo—"

"What the bloody hell is going on here?" A man in his fifties strode out of the field beyond the barn. He wore wellingtons, into which he had tucked his loose-fitting trousers, and a dark blue jumper that looked like it had been repaired on more than a few occasions during its lifetime. His hair had receded to no more than a patch above his ears, the rest of his scalp an angry red where it had been caught by the sun. The same angry red, along with a matching expression, coloured his face.

"Now you've done it," Wendy whispered.

"Wendy, get back inside." He waved her in, and she complied, disappearing through the doorway and closing the door behind her.

"What are you doing on my farm?" he said, directing his attention toward Kate.

"We're looking for a missing boy," Kate said.

"There's no missing boy here. Now get off my property."

"Have you seen this boy come this way?" Kate showed him the photograph. "His name is Michael Roberts. He's twelve years old." She was hoping to appeal to the man's better nature by mentioning Michael's young age but realised even as she said it that she was probably wasting her time.

"Haven't seen him, never heard of him. Now get off my land. You're trespassing."

Kate sighed. They weren't going to get any answers here. "All right, sir, we'll leave. But could you keep an eye out for Michael? He's missing and his parents are worried about him." There she went again, trying to reach a spark of humanity in the man who stood before her. "I'm sure if it was Charlie who was missing, you'd-_"

"Charlie isn't missing, and I don't know anything about this Roberts boy. You need to get off my farm."

"We came that way," Kaye said, indicating the gate. "Through your field."

"So, you climbed the bloody fence as well, did you? Well, if that's the way you came, that's the way you can leave."

There was nothing to be gained here. Not at the moment, anyway. "All right." Kate walked to the gate, which Dalton opened. Kate could feel the man's eyes boring into her back as she stepped through and entered the field.

"He's a nasty piece of work," Dalton said when they were out of earshot. "It's not hard to see what's going on there. His wife looked like a deer caught in headlights. She's terrified of her husband."

"If he *is* her husband," Kate said. "We have no way of knowing that yet."

"Yet?" Dalton grinned. "So, you're going to do a bit of digging?"

Kate nodded. "Of course."

They reached the fence and climbed over. Kate cast a glance back at the farmhouse. The man stood at the top of the field, hands on his hips, watching her.

CHAPTER
NINE

TOM SAT HEAVILY on the hillside, gasping for breath. He had just called for another break because he wasn't sure he could ascend any farther up Stone Peak unless he rested his aching muscles and waited for his hammering heart to slow down.

He fished the walkie talkie out of his rucksack and pressed the button a couple of times. "DS Ryan, are you there? Over."

A hiss of static came out of the speaker, then Ryan's voice, sounding distant, said, "Here, guv. We're conducting the search of the woods and we've spoken to the residents of a nearby farm. I'll let you know about that later. Nothing to report regarding Michael yet. Over."

"We found something that might be of interest," he said, "but no sign of Michael here either."

"Something that might be of interest?"

"A plastic container buried in the hillside. Forensics are on their way to dig it up. It might be nothing."

"Or it could be the lead we need." She didn't sound hopeful, but it was hard to tell through the static.

"We'll see. Speak to you later. Over and out."

He replaced the walkie talkie in the rucksack and took out a bottle of water, which he drank from before closing his eyes and pouring some over his face. With his eyes still closed, he leaned back on his elbows, the breeze cooling his wet skin.

"Excuse me, sir."

Tom opened his eyes and looked up at a burly, dark-haired officer. "What is it?"

"I don't think the boy could have gone any further this way, sir. And neither can we. Not without climbing gear, anyway." He gestured up the slope.

Tom got to his feet and turned around. A hundred feet above where he stood, a sheer rock face rose out of the ground, blocking the way to the summit. The almost-vertical wall of rock was at least thirty feet high. The officer was right; there was no way Michael had gone any farther than this spot, if he'd ever been on this part of the Peak at all.

A sinking feeling entered Tom's gut. All this effort in vain. Unless Ryan's team found anything, today was a failure. Nothing to show for all their hard work except a plastic box that might be nothing at all. It might contain nothing more than the remains of a climber's sandwiches.

Evening was closing in. The wind had brought dark

clouds from the north. They hung over Stone Peak like a shroud.

Tomorrow, both teams would search the other fork of the trail; the section that wound around the base of the Peak to the West. But until then, they were no closer to finding Michael. If the boy was alive, he was going to have to spend a second night out in the open.

That thought sparked another that Tom liked even less. What if Michael wasn't out in the wilds at all? What if he was being held somewhere against his will?

It was a possibility he had to consider.

"All right," he said. "We're going back down."

The officer nodded and returned to his place in the search line.

"We can't go any farther," Tom said, raising his voice so everyone could hear him. "We're returning to the vehicles. Good job, everyone. Keep your eyes peeled on the way down. You never know, we might have missed something on the way up."

An affirmative murmur rose from the troops as well as some sighs of relief. Getting up here hadn't been easy. It had taken its toll on everyone, Tom included.

"Be careful on the way down," he added, looking at the steep descent to the trail below.

He picked his way carefully around crags and gullies as he descended, the growing gloom making it difficult to see. Spots of rain began to fall, spattering off the rocks. Petrichor rose from the ground, its earthy aroma assaulting Tom's nostrils.

This is how it should be, Tom thought. *It should be rain-*

ing. Sunny days are happy days, and this is not a happy day. The skies are dark, and rightly so. There should be a sense of hopelessness.

When he got to the place where the plastic container had been found, a SOCO in a white Tyvek suit was there, on her hands and knees in the wet gully.

Tom stopped and waited a short distance away, thankful for the rain as it cooled him down.

The Scenes of Crimes Officer worked meticulously, finally freeing the box from the dirt. After brushing mud from the container, she bagged it and held it up to the dimming light.

Tom got closer and peered in through the box's clear plastic sides. Whatever was in there was wrapped in a piece of bright red cloth.

"We'll open it back at the lab," the SOCO said. "There would be all sorts of cross-contamination if we opened it out here in this weather."

Tom nodded, frustrated but understanding. "Let me know as soon as you find out what's in there."

Taking his phone from his pocket, he photographed the hole in the soil where the Tupperware container had been buried and also took a couple of shots from a wider angle to get a more accurate indication of the place where the buried container had been found.

He had no idea if the item that had just been bagged was related to Michael and Sam, but it was damn strange that it was buried here, almost directly above the place where it looked like the boys' bikes had been lying in the mud.

When he got back to the parking area, it was fully dark. Tom drank another bottle of water, sitting in his car as he poured the liquid down his throat. The tedious descent down Stone Peak had set his thigh muscles on fire, and sitting in the comfy car seat felt like heaven after sitting on rocks and grass all day. The rainfall had become a downpour. It hissed down onto the car roof and smeared across the windscreen.

The officers were climbing into the van, more than ready to go home and get some rest.

It was too late to begin a search of the unexplored section of the trail. That would have to wait until tomorrow. There was no point doing a half-arsed job in the dark and the rain, with tired police officers who could only concentrate on their next meal or daydream about getting some shuteye.

Tom realised he hadn't eaten anything since the porridge he'd had for breakfast that morning. Not the greatest idea on a day like today.

The police van left the parking area and drove past the reporters who were still stationed across the road, hungry for any titbit of a story, despite the weather.

Tom supposed he should check in with Ryan. He had expected her and Team Bravo to show up by now, but there was no sign of them. If they hadn't found anything in the woods, it was time to call them back. Their efforts could be put to better use tomorrow. The as yet unexplored area around the other side of the Peak might prove more fruitful.

But what exactly were they looking for at this point? If Michael was still alive, why hadn't he returned home? He might be stuck somewhere —in a ravine with a broken leg, or on a rocky crag he couldn't get down from— but that meant his chances of survival were low. He'd been out here for twenty-four hours now, exposed to throat-parching heat in the day and colder temperatures at night. The boy's chances of survival dwindled with each passing minute.

Tom reached into the backseat and opened his rucksack. He took out the map he'd been carrying —a detailed map of Stone Peak and the surrounding area— and laid it out on the steering wheel, tracing his finger along the trail from the parking area. When he reached the fork where Ryan and her team had moved north to the woods, he continued west, around the base of the hill.

He wasn't an expert navigator, but he reckoned an hour's walk would take him a good distance along that part of the trail. There was no light left, and the rain was coming down like something out of the Epic of Gilgamesh, but he had a powerful torch in the boot. He also had the waterproof jacket his father had given him that morning.

Finishing the water, he slipped two more bottles into his rucksack, along with the map.

He hesitated for a moment, wondering if what he was about to do was crazy, or even dangerous.

Then he thought about the grinning boy in the photograph —standing by the river with his now-dead friend— and imagined that boy lost somewhere out there in the rainy night.

Climbing out of the car, Tom hefted the pack onto his shoulders and set off along the trail at a determined pace.

CHAPTER TEN

THE SEARCH of the woods hadn't delivered anything useful, and now the heavens had broken, casting a deluge of rain down onto the trees. It hit the foliage above Kate's head, splashing off the leaves and dripping down to the ground. Standing beneath it was like standing in a shower.

Kate pulled the waterproof jacket from her rucksack and put it on. It was getting dark now, and although she hated to admit defeat, it was time to call the search off.

She called Michael's name for what seemed like the thousandth time. And just like the nine-hundred and ninety-nine times before, there was no reply.

Her thoughts kept returning to the people at the farm. The sunburned man had been keen to get her and PC Dalton off his property, which might be understandable, but there was a missing twelve-year-old boy's life at stake; surely anyone would want to help find him, even a farmer who liked his privacy.

And why was privacy so important to the man? A lot of people in rural areas liked to keep themselves to themselves, but was there more to it than that? Did the sunburned man have something to hide?

Kate knew it was wrong to jump to conclusions, especially in a case like this, but the family dynamic she had witnessed at the farm left her feeling uneasy.

Her walkie talkie crackled. "You there, Ryan? Over."

She hoped Brand was calling her because he'd found Michael. She pressed the button.

"Ryan here, guv. Over."

"Anything to report?"

"Not unless you're a birdwatcher. We've seen plenty of those."

"I've stood Alpha Team down. I suggest you do the same. We'll have another crack at it tomorrow."

Kate pursed her lips and nodded.

"You there, Ryan?"

"I'm here. It's just that the day hasn't ended the way I expected." She'd wanted to find Michael so badly that she'd managed to convince herself he would come home today. This wasn't a job well done. They'd been out here all day and were no closer to finding him than they had been this morning.

There was a pause, and then the DI said, "I'm taking a walk around the Peak. You're welcome to join me, if you want."

"In this weather?"

"You don't have to come if you don't want to."

"I'm coming," she said. "You're from the city;

someone has to make sure you don't get lost out there." As soon as the words left her lips, she cringed inwardly. She shouldn't be speaking to her guv'nor like that.

Brand seemed not to notice. He simply said, "All right. Send the team home and I'll meet you at the junction where the trail heads west."

"Will do. Over and out." She put the walkie talkie away quickly and addressed the team. "Good work, everyone. We're going to call it a day."

She sensed disappointment coming from the officers. Despite the fact that it was now nighttime and raining, they were determined to find Michael.

"I appreciate your effort, and I'm sure Michael will too, when he finds out about it. But for now, we have to be sensible. We'll try again tomorrow."

She called Michael's name one last time and waited for a response. Wind whispered through the trees and birds sang and argued, but there was no sign of a lost boy who might have wandered into these woods after witnessing the death of his friend.

She led the officers back the way they had come, out of the woods and south towards Stone Peak. The high hill sat stoically in the landscape, rising above everything else like a guardian of stone. Whatever it had witnessed yesterday, it was not about to tell.

DI Brand was waiting for her at the trail junction, standing with his hood up and head bowed against the onslaught of rain. Kate approached him, the officers assembling behind her.

"Get some rest," she said to the team, "and something to eat. We'll be out here bright and early tomorrow."

The officers set off down the path that led to the parking area, whispering among themselves. Kate knew that she and the DI were the subject of those whispers. Anything out of the ordinary, like the DI and DS sending the officers home while they stayed on the trail, was fair game for gossip.

"Right," she said. "We're going for a walk, are we?"

Brand nodded. "I thought we might see how far we can get around the hill in an hour."

Kate glanced at the route ahead. The rain wasn't letting up anytime soon. It had churned the trail into a muddy quagmire teeming with puddles.

She'd told her team they had to be sensible. Was *this* sensible? Going for a nighttime walk around Stone Peak?

Michael might be out there somewhere, she told herself. If the poor boy was surviving in the wilds, then she could endure an hour or two of hardship to look for him, no matter how hungry and tired she felt.

"This is tomorrow's search area, isn't it?" she said to Brand.

"It is."

"So, we're getting an early start?"

"This isn't an official search. We're just going for a stroll."

"But if we happen to find Michael…"

"…then we happen to find Michael."

"I like it."

"Then let's go."

They started along the trail, Stone Peak looming on their left in the darkness. Brand's torch cut through the night, illuminating the line of mud snaking through the grass that was the trail; a line of hard-packed dirt only an hour ago, now almost sunken and lost.

Again, Kate questioned if this was a good idea and again, she steeled herself with the thought that a twelve-year-old boy could be out here, struggling to survive in the rain, the cold, and the night. How scared must he be feeling right now?

Brand swept the torch beam to either side of the trail at regular intervals. Kate followed the light and squinted against the rain as she inspected the revealed landscape for a shape that didn't belong, something that might indicate Michael had been here, or was here now. The light illuminated lonely trees, empty fields, and the forbidding slope of Stone Peak, but nothing else.

"You said you spoke to some people earlier," the DI said after a while.

"There's a farm near the woods," Kate replied. "The family that lives there are called the Gibbons, I think. Wendy Gibbon was scared as soon as she saw us, adamant that they knew nothing about Michael. Her husband —if it *was* her husband— was furious that we were on his land. Sent us packing as soon as he knew we were there."

"Could be nothing," Brand said. "A lot of the farmers around here are like that."

"It could be nothing," she agreed, "or it could be something. I'd at least like to know the man's name."

In the darkness, she couldn't see if the DI nodded or not. His face was lost beneath his hood. Finally, he said, "No harm in that. But don't try to get a search warrant just yet."

"Oh, I'm much sneakier than that, guv. If I was at the point of searching the man's farm, I'd already have an airtight case against him."

He laughed. It was short and pleasant-sounding.

They walked in silence after that, assailed by the relentless rain as they searched as much of the area as they could in the circumstances. The task would be a hundred times easier in the morning, Kate knew, but she also understood why they were out here in the dark. Brand was just as invested in finding Michael Roberts as she was. Another mental tick went into the 'good boss' column of her tally sheet. So far, the Detective Inspector was winning her over.

Finally, after they'd been trudging through the mud for an hour, Brand halted and checked his watch. He turned to Kate so she could see his face beneath his hood. His features looked grim in the torchlight. "I think we're going to have to call it a day."

She nodded, realising the import of what passed unspoken between them: Michael was going to have to spend another night out here alone.

Together, they turned and retraced their muddy steps.

As the rain battered Kate's face, it tasted of bitter defeat.

———

When they got back to the cars, Kate was shivering. Her jacket had kept most of the rain away from her body, but her wet trousers clung to her legs. Rainwater and mud had found their way into her boots —the result of stepping into puddles that came up over her boot tops— and chilled her feet.

Her suitcase was still in the boot of her car, but she wasn't about to change here, in the car park.

The DI was in a similar state. Mud covered his trousers and boots, and when he took off his jacket and stuffed it into the boot of his car, it was obvious that some of the rain had found its way inside the jacket and soaked his jumper.

"See you in the morning," he said, closing the boot.

"See you tomorrow, guv." She slid into the driver's seat of her car and turned the engine on, cranking the heater up as far as it would go. She sat there shivering, waiting for the engine to heat up and send warm air through the vents.

A sudden knock on the window startled her. The DI was out there, shielding his eyes from the rain with his hand.

Kate rolled the window down.

"Do you have somewhere to go?" he asked. "To eat, I mean."

"I'm staying at a B&B in the village," she told him. "I've got a packet of crisps and half a ham sandwich I bought from a garage this morning."

"I'm making dinner for my dad. You're welcome to join us."

A warm meal or a stale sandwich? It was a no-brainer. "Of course, guv. Thanks."

"Right. Follow me." He ran back to his car and started the engine.

Kate rolled up the window against the night and waited for the DI to make a move. He reversed out of his parking spot and made his way slowly and carefully onto the road. The reporters had all gone home now, their search for the truth washed away by the rain.

Kate followed the DI's car out of the parking area. When she was half a mile down the road, looking forward to a meal that would stop her stomach rumbling, and also finding out more about the enigmatic DI Tom Brand, she stopped shivering as the vents finally did what they were supposed to, and started throwing warm air into the car.

CHAPTER
ELEVEN

TOM PARKED outside his dad's house and waited for DS Ryan to arrive. When he'd asked her to dine with him and his dad, it had been an impulsive action, something he'd done almost without thinking. He'd had time to mull it over on the way here. A Detective Inspector inviting a Detective Sergeant to his house for dinner might be frowned on by the higher-ups. People like DCI Holt, or Tom's old boss in London would take a dim view of such fraternisation.

But Kate Ryan had done a good job today. Tom could see the kind of person she was —driven, and willing to put in the work even if it meant going above and beyond the call of duty— and the thought of her eating nothing more than a sandwich and crisps, alone in a B&B, after a day like today, didn't sit right with him.

The DS's green Jeep pulled up next to Tom's Saab and the headlights died as she stopped the engine.

The front door opened. His father stood there, silhouetted against the light spilling out of the house. "Come inside. You'll catch your death out there."

Tom entered the house, gesturing for Ryan to follow him. She rushed around to her boot and hefted a suitcase out of it before running into the house. She smiled at Tom's dad as she stood in the hallway with her hair plastered to her face, looking like a drowned rat.

"This is DS Ryan, Dad," Tom said.

"Call me Kate." She said, reaching out and shaking hands.

"I'm Max," Tom's dad said.

She frowned. "Wait a minute. Max Brand. Are you DCI Brand from the Buxton station?"

"I used to be," he said, obviously pleased she'd heard of him. "I'm retired now. My garden keeps me busy enough these days. Well, get changed and come through to the living room. I'll get a fire going so you can warm up. You both look like you've been wrestling alligators in a swamp." He disappeared into the living room.

Tom took his boots off, struggling with the wet laces. The DS followed suit and placed her boots neatly by the front door. She hung her waterproof jacket on the coat stand.

"You can change in there," Tom said, indicating the downstairs bathroom. "There are fresh towels in the cupboard."

He went upstairs to find some dry clothes and freshen up.

The downstairs bathroom was much more spacious than Kate had expected, with enough room for her to place the suitcase on the edge of the corner bath and position herself in front of a large mirror above the sink.

The rain at the Peak had been the type of downpour that somehow manages to get through waterproof clothing, and it had soaked her hair and face. She found a pile of fresh, folded towels in the cupboard and used one to gently rub the long, wet tendrils of hair that had stuck to her face and neck.

She peeled off her wet clothes and found a dry pair of jeans and a black turtleneck sweater in the suitcase. Once they were on, she felt warm and comfortable.

She left the bathroom in search of Max and DI Brand. The house was large enough to be comfortable yet small enough to be cosy. The decor was rustic cottage style, with exposed beams and a big stone fireplace in the living room.

Max was in the living room, in front the fireplace, steadily blowing at a pile of kindling in the grate, trying to get it to light. The glowing embers crackled into life and the pleasant scent of cedar smoke drifted into the room. Max placed a log from a pile next to the hearth onto the burgeoning flames and nodded, seemingly satisfied.

"This will get you warmed up in no time." He climbed shakily to his feet and stood back, giving Kate room to stand by the fire. "You don't mind if I sit down, do you, Kate? I'm not as steady on my feet as I used to be."

"Of course not," she said. "Have you lived here long? The house is lovely."

"Forty years. I can't take any credit for the decor; that was all my wife's doing." He smiled, but Kate saw sadness glisten in his eyes.

Attempting to steer the conversation away from what was obviously a sore point, she nodded at the windows, which were awash with rain. "Crazy weather we're having. A beautiful summer's day one minute, and now this."

"I expect it's playing havoc with your search efforts."

"It doesn't make things any easier, that's for sure."

Brand arrived into the room, dressed in a fresh pair of jeans and a dark blue, crew neck sweater. "How does spaghetti bolognese sound? It's all I could find in the cupboards."

"That sounds amazing," Kate said. He could have said beans on toast, and she would have appreciated it just as much. She had simple tastes when it came to food, and she certainly wouldn't say no to spagbol.

The DI went into the kitchen. The sounds of

cupboards opening and pots and pans clattering ensued.

"We'd better go in there and keep him company," Max said, getting up from the sofa.

Kate followed him into a kitchen decorated in the same rustic style as the rest of the house. Pine cupboards, a pine table that looked like it had sat there for many years, and a sash window that looked out over a garden. It was too dark to see much out there, and rain ran down the outside of the glass in wide rivulets, but Kate guessed the garden was just as lovely as the house.

Brand was fussing with pots and pans, heating up water for the pasta and arranging jars of basil and oregano on the counter, as well as salt, pepper, and half a dozen ripe, red tomatoes.

"You're making the sauce from scratch?" Kate said. Whenever she had pasta, she used sauce from a jar.

"Is there any other way?" the DI said.

"Yes, there are things called jars. They sell them in supermarkets."

"But they don't taste as good as this."

"The tomatoes are from the greenhouse," Max said from his seat at the table. "Did you know my son was an accomplished cook, Kate?"

"I had no idea."

"He learned at an early age, and he's enjoyed it ever since."

"It's a useful skill," she said. "One that I don't

possess, I'm afraid. My tea usually consists of beans on toast or a pot noodle."

Max grinned. "I know what it's like when you're working all hours; sometimes that's all you've got the energy for. I'm much the same, to be honest. If it wasn't for Tom being here, I'd probably be tucking into a bowl of chicken soup right about now."

"That's why you need me here, Dad. Someone's got to feed you up," the DI said, mixing the ingredients of the sauce together in a saucepan.

The light-hearted banter continued while the meal was being prepared. It was easy to see the warmth between father and son. Kate found herself smiling at the exchanges between them. Max recounted stories of his son's childhood. Like the time Tom climbed an apple tree in the garden to eat the fruit and then fell out of the tree and broke his arm. He ended up in the hospital with his arm in a cast and a stomach ache.

Or how, when he was nine, the DI decided he was going to be a stunt rider and built a ramp in the back garden out of plywood and old milk crates. His first attempt at performing a daring jump off the ramp had resulted in yet another broken arm, as well as damage to his bike.

As the conversation went on, the smell of basil, oregano, and tomato drifted from the pan on the stove, and Kate's stomach rumbled in anticipation.

When Tom brought the food over to the table and served the pasta and sauce, the conversation stopped and everyone ate in silence, which Kate was glad about because she didn't want to talk. Talking meant she would have to stop eating, and the bolognese the DI had made was the best she'd ever tasted anywhere.

When she was finished, she nodded in appreciation and said to Brand, "That was amazing. Thank you."

He smiled and collected the plates from the table.

"Let me wash up," Kate said. "It's the least I can do."

The DI opened a cupboard door to reveal a built-in dishwasher. "No need for that."

His phone, which had been sitting on the counter while he was cooking, buzzed. Brand answered it. "DI Brand." There was a pause and then he said, "Okay, what have you got?" He went silent for a moment, nodding as he listened to the voice on the other end. "I see. Send me a photo, I'd like to have a look at it. And you're analysing the cloth as well, right? Okay. Thanks, bye."

He placed the phone back on the counter and turned to face Max and Kate. "That was Sheila at the lab. She's opened the Tupperware box. There was a necklace inside, wrapped in a piece of red velvet."

His phone *dinged*. He picked it up and stared at the screen for a moment before passing it to Kate.

The photo showed a gold necklace laid out on a white surface, the lab's ruler lying next to it to denote size. Next to the necklace lay a piece of red velvet with ragged edges, as if it had been cut roughly from a larger piece of fabric.

The piece of jewellery didn't look particularly

remarkable in any way, certainly not remarkable enough to be buried in a hillside. The chain was thin and delicate with a gold pendant shaped like a sun, with stylised wavy tendrils radiating from the central circle to suggest rays.

"Strange thing to bury on Stone Peak," the DI said.

Kate simply nodded. She didn't know what to say. It was a strange thing to bury on Stone Peak, and she wondered how a piece of jewellery like this could possibly be connected to Michael and Sam. Nothing sprang to mind.

She sighed heavily. They were still no closer to finding Michael or discovering what had happened on the riverbank yesterday.

TUESDAY

CHAPTER
TWELVE

THE NEXT MORNING, Tom ran the gauntlet of reporters outside the station and found DS Ryan in the inner office, tapping away at a keyboard while the search teams from yesterday milled about around her.

"Listen up," Tom said. "Today we are going to search the area where the trail curves around Stone Peak to the west. You will all be working together as one unit. I need someone to coordinate the search. Any volunteers?"

A tall, female PC with blonde plaits tucked under her hat raised her hand. "I volunteer, sir. PC Dalton."

"All right, everyone, PC Dalton is in charge. Report any finds to her. Good luck out there. Let's try to bring Michael home today."

The officers left the station. Kate got up from the desk, eyebrows raised questioningly. "Aren't we joining them?"

"There's something else we need to do first. I want

to have a word with the people who live in those houses near the Peak." He gestured to the map of the area. "When you mentioned the farmer yesterday—"

"George Gibbon," she said. "I just found his name the database. Not surprisingly, he's had some run-ins with the law in the past."

Tom dipped his head to the map, pointing at a cluster of buildings. "This is his farm here. But he's not the only landowner in the area. There's a house to the east, and another down here, in this valley to the west. The people in those dwellings are just as likely to have seen Michael as the Gibbon family, and we might get some civil answers out of them."

"So, we're not going after George?"

Her disappointed tone made him laugh. "Going after him? On what grounds? We can't shoot him just because he was rude. This isn't Dirty Harry, Ryan."

He said that last comment with a mock serious expression on his face and now it was her turn to laugh.

"I didn't mean shoot him, exactly. Maybe just rough him up a bit."

They both laughed at that. Tom brought his attention to the map again. "This farm in the east is owned by a Wesley Brady, who lives with his partner Diane Summers. We'll start there and then move to the western farm which is owned by Henry and Lois Farrow."

"I just hope we get a slightly warmer reception than the one I got at the Gibbon place."

"That remains to be seen. After we talk to these

people, we're going to see Peggy Jones and the Roberts family They both have Family Liaison Officers assigned to them, but I want to visit them personally, let them know we haven't forgotten about them."

"Of course."

"Perhaps we'll even have some good news, if the search team finds Michael." But even as he said the words, he could hear how flat they sounded. They dropped heavily into the space between him and Ryan. Did he believe Michael Roberts was still alive? It was a question he didn't like to consider, because he knew the odds of finding the boy alive and well at this point were so low that even the most desperate gambler wouldn't take a chance on them.

If Michael was out there alone, it was likely he had perished from exposure. If he *wasn't* alone, the chances of him being found alive were so slim they almost wasted away to nothing.

DS Ryan, who was no fool and probably shared similar thoughts, merely nodded.

"We'll take my car," Tom said, changing the subject so he didn't have to dwell on it any longer.

The road outside the station was quiet for a change. The press vehicles and reporters had obviously gone after the search team. Not in search of a lost boy but pursuing a story to headline their papers and collect clicks on the Internet.

The rain had stopped sometime during the night, leaving a slick sheen over the roads and darkening the trees.

As he got into his car, Tom fiddled with the Satnav, trying to find the Brady farm in the database. The computer didn't seem to have a clue that the farm existed at all.

"I know the way," Ryan said, after watching him struggle with the damned thing. "Well, I can get us to the general vicinity, anyway. We should be able to find it from there."

Tom nodded, thankful she was a local. Without her, he'd probably be driving aimlessly around back roads all day, getting nowhere.

They found the Brady farm after a short search, during which Tom had let the DS guide him down farm tracks and narrow roads of hard-packed dirt until they finally found a sign reading *Brady Farm* on a low stone wall, next to a metal gate. Ryan opened the gate and Tom drove through. A short track led them to a neat house with outbuildings behind it, surrounded by fields of cows and sheep.

As they got out of the car, a heavyset, grey-haired man in wellingtons and dark blue overalls came around the side of the house, wiping his hands on a rag, which he pushed into the pocket of the grease-stained overalls. The man's bare forearms were similarly stained.

"Morning," He nodded at them and waited for them to speak.

Tom took his warrant card out of his pocket and showed it to the man. "Detective Inspector Brand from the Derbyshire Constabulary. This is my partner, Detective Sergeant Ryan. I was wondering if we could have a word with you about a boy who's gone missing in the area."

"I heard about that. One of them was found in the river, wasn't he? A rum do."

Tom wasn't familiar with the expression. "Are you Wesley Brady?"

"That's me. Not sure how I can help you, Detective Inspector. We're miles away from the river here."

"We're looking for anyone who might have seen Michael Roberts. It's possible he came this way. Have you seen a young boy on your land at all?"

Wesley shook his head. "Can't say I have. Mind you, there's a lot of places he could be around here. The woods are easy to get lost in. Or if not lost, the boy could be hiding in there."

"Hiding?" Ryan asked.

Wesley shrugged. "Probably had a falling out with his parents and ran away with his friend. Then the friend falls in the river and drowns so the poor lad panics and hides."

"You seem to have given this some thought," Tom said.

"I was watching it on the news with my partner. We talked about it, that's all."

"Is your partner here?"

As if on cue, the front door opened and a grey-haired woman in dark blue trousers and a white summer top waved at them. "Come inside, the tea is brewing."

Wesley rolled his eyes. "That's my missus, always welcoming strangers into the house. That's how we ended up with so many bloody stray cats. Now the barn is full of kittens."

"Come in, come in." The woman ushered them into a kitchen where the smell of tea and freshly baked biscuits made Tom's stomach rumble, despite the fact he'd had porridge and toast for breakfast only a few hours ago.

"I'm Diane," the woman said. "Take a seat. I can guess what brings you to our neck of the woods." She went to the counter and brought a bone China tea pot over to the kitchen table. Tom and Ryan sat as she served them tea in matching cups.

"It's that poor boy, isn't it?" she said as she put a milk pitcher and sugar bowl on the table next to the pot. "You still haven't found him. We were watching it on the news. Terrible business. Simply terrible."

"You haven't seen him, have you?" Tom asked as he added milk and sugar to his cup.

She looked shocked at the suggestion. "Seen him? Why would I have seen him?"

"He could have come this way. The trail that leads from the river skirts one of your fields."

"Oh, I see. You think he's come along the trail. Well,

we wouldn't see him from the house in that case. There are trees in the way. You might try George Gibbons' old barn. That's in the field next to ours."

"I don't think the lad will be in there," Wesley said.

"You never know." Diane shot a look at an enigmatic look at Wesley before returning her attention to Tom. "It isn't far from the river, and it's hidden in an overgrown field. It's falling apart, so anyone can get in. George should have it pulled down, to be honest. It's dangerous."

"I'll look into it," Tom said. He took a sip of the tea. It was scalding hot but brewed to perfection. "Are there any outbuildings her that you don't use much? Is it possible Michael could be hiding in one of them?"

"We've only got the old cow barn, and the car shed," Wesley said. "And there's nothing in the barn except a mother cat and her kittens. As for the car shed, there's no boy in there. I was in there before you arrived, working on the engine of my Scimitar."

"A Scimitar?" Tom was going to ask if he could have a look around but now, he saw an easier way to do that. "I haven't seen one of those in years."

"Well, you're welcome to have a look once you finish your tea," Wesley said. "I keep her in good working order. She's a beauty."

"Those cars are his pride and joy," Diane said. "He loves them more than he does me."

Wesley chuckled. "You know that isn't true, love. Come on, Inspector, I'll show you the car shed. And we can have a look in the barn as well while we're at it, just to prove there isn't a lost lad hiding in there."

He took them outside to the back yard, which was flanked by a wooden barn and a long, brick building with wide double doors that had been painted red.

Three cars sat inside: a green Land Rover Defender, which was covered with mud and looked like Wesley's work vehicle; a black SUV, which was probably used for tasks like going into town and shopping; and a russet-coloured Reliant Scimitar which was parked over a pit that allowed access to the car's undercarriage.

Tools and tyres occupied every available space on the walls and floor. The smell of rubber and oil filled the air.

Tom could see how much love and care Wesley had put into this space. Except for the muddy Land Rover, everything gleamed.

"Here she is." Wesley gestured to the Scimitar with a proud glint in his eyes.

"She's lovely, all right." Tom made a show of inspecting the car's lines while, out of the corner of his eye, he checked the garage for places a twelve-year-old boy might hide. DS Ryan, out of Wesley's line of sight, was more blatant in her search efforts, leaning around piles of tyres to check what was behind them and even crouching down to check underneath the Land Rover and the SUV.

After making what he considered to be an adequate fuss over the car, Tom said, "Is the barn as neat as this?"

Taking the hint, Wesley said, "All right, Inspector,

we'll have a look at the barn. Lucy might not be too happy about it, but she'll just have to live with it."

"Lucy?"

"The cat."

"Ah, right."

They crossed the yard to the barn, a large building with stalls for cattle and a ladder that led up to a hayloft.

If I were a twelve-year-old boy looking for a place to hide, Tom thought, *this would be perfect.*

"Do you mind if we look around?"

The farmer gestured at the spacious area. "Look wherever you like, but I'm telling you there's no boy in there."

"And where is Lucy?" Ryan asked.

"Third stall on the left."

The detectives entered the barn, Ryan peeking into the stalls while Tom moved to the ladder. He reckoned the hayloft would be the best place for Michael to hide, if he was in here at all. As he stepped onto the first rickety wooden rung, he heard it creak beneath his weight.

Everything will be fine. Wesley must use this ladder all the time, and he looks much heavier than me.

"Do you go up to the hayloft often?" he asked the farmer as he gingerly climbed another couple of creaking rungs.

"No," Wesley said. "I don't trust that ladder. You'll be all right, though, Inspector. There's barely an ounce of fat on you."

That didn't fill Tom with confidence. He held the sides of the ladder tightly as he continued upwards.

When he got to the top, he breathed a sigh of relief and pulled himself up into the loft, which consisted of a simple boarded floor and not much else. A couple of pitchforks rested against the wall, and that was it. There was nowhere for a mouse to hide, much less a boy.

He heard voices below. Wesley was speaking to another man. Tom couldn't make out any words; his pulse was still pounding in his ears from climbing the ladder. He risked a glance down to the floor below and immediately wished he hadn't.

He took a deep breath and lowered himself back onto the top rung of the ladder, grimacing as it creaked in protest. He descended as quickly as he could and let out a long breath when he finally reached the floor.

DS Ryan was coming from the rear of the barn, shaking her head. "Nothing here, guv."

Wesley was standing in the sunlight outside the door, speaking to a man in his twenties. The man wore a tan baseball cap, jeans, and a *Fortnite* T-shirt.

"That's Charlie Gibbon," Ryan whispered. "George Gibbon's son."

Wesley poked his head in through the door. "Is it all right if Charlie comes in now? He's come to see the kittens."

"Of course," Tom said, waving the young man inside.

Charlie Gibbon entered the barn and went over to the stall where the mother cat and her litter of kittens were resting on a bed of straw. His face lit up as he watched them.

"Charlie has been here every day since the kittens were born," Wesley said. "He's looking out for them, aren't you, Charlie?"

Charlie nodded, his eyes never leaving the stall's occupants.

"That's good," Tom said, joining the young man. "You're from the farm next door aren't you, Charlie? Did you drive here?"

The young man laughed, a quick guffaw. "No, I don't drive."

"So you walked. That's good exercise. Must be a long way from your house to here."

Charlie shrugged. "I don't mind. I like to see the kittens."

"Of course you do. Do you go walking a lot?"

"Every day."

"Do you go walking by the river?"

"I like the river. But I mustn't get too close. I have to stay on the path."

"That's a good rule to follow. Very sensible. Did you go to the river two days ago?" Tom wondered if Charlie might be a potential witness. If he'd seen the boys at the river, he might have seen someone else there as well.

Charlie frowned. "I don't know."

"Charlie, we're looking for two boys. They were at the river two days ago. Perhaps you saw them there."

"Do you mean Michael and Sam?"

"You know them?"

Charlie nodded enthusiastically. "They're my friends."

Tom paused and watched the kittens crawling on the hay for a moment. He had no idea how much Charlie knew regarding the fate of Sam Jones and the disappearance of Michael Roberts. He didn't want to upset the young man by revealing bad news.

"When did you last see your friends?"

"I don't know."

"Okay, that's fine. Can you remember what they were doing the last time you saw them?"

Charlie nodded. "They were solving a mystery."

"A mystery?"

"They're detectives."

"Yes, I heard that. What mystery were they solving?"

"I don't know. They wouldn't tell me. Sam said if he told me, it wouldn't be a mystery anymore."

"I see. And where were you when he told you that?"

"On the trail."

"Near the river?"

"I think so."

"So they were solving a mystery at the river."

"No, not at the river. The mystery was somewhere else. I wasn't allowed to go there because they said you have to be very quiet to solve a mystery, and I'm not always quiet."

"Ah, I see. So, they left you at the river and they went somewhere else."

"I don't mind. I like to be on my own sometimes."

"Of course. We all like to be alone every now and then. So, if you were friends with Michael and Sam, that means you probably saw them quite a lot."

Charlie simply nodded.

"Was there ever anybody else there with them?"

"No."

"Who else do you see on the trail? You probably know a lot of people."

"Some people talk to me and some people don't."

"I see. What about the people you talk to? Who are they?"

"Charlie and Bess. And Mr Barker."

"Charlie and Bess," Tom said. "Same name as you."

"Yes, but I'm Charlie Gibbon and he's Charlie Lewis. Bess is his dog. She's fluffy."

"I think I've met Charlie and Bess," Tom said, remembering the dog walker who had found Sam's body. "Who is Mr Barker?"

"He walks his dog, and he takes photographs. His dog's name is Fred."

"And does he speak to you? Mr Barker, I mean, not Fred."

Charlie laughed. "Fred can't talk because he's a dog. Mr Barker shows me the photographs he takes sometimes. They're trees and grass and things like that. Sometimes they have people in them, but there isn't any colour and they're boring. I tell Mr Barker I like them, though, because if I told him they're boring, he'd be sad."

"That's very wise of you. Does he talk to Michael

and Sam? Perhaps he shows *them* his photographs as well."

"I don't think so. I've never seen him talking to them."

"Well, thank you, Charlie. You've been a big help."

Charlie turned to face Tom for the first time. "Are you a policeman?"

"I'm a detective."

"Like Michael and Sam."

"Yes."

Charlie went back to watching the kittens in the stall.

"We're going to go now," Tom said, "but thanks again." He walked past Charlie to where Wesley stood by the barn door.

"If he knows anything more than what he just told you, Inspector," Wesley said, "I reckon it's locked up in his head. You'll not get any more out of the lad."

When they were back in the car, Ryan said, "Looks like we've got a lead. Shouldn't be too difficult to track down this Mr Barker."

Tom's stomach rumbled. He checked his watch. "Let's get some lunch before we talk to the Farrows. What's the pub in Relby like for food?"

"The Mermaid? Quite good."

"Right, let's grab a bite there. I'm buying."

He needed time to mull over the information he'd been given by Charlie Gibbon, and food helped him think more clearly.

CHAPTER
THIRTEEN

THE MERMAID PUB WAS BUSTLING. Kate spotted a table in the corner and grabbed it while Brand went to the bar to order two shepherd's pies, the Meal of the Day. While she waited, Kate checked the pub for journalists. The clientele consisted mostly of hikers and tourists, with a few locals enjoying a pint at the bar. The reporters were probably still at the search site, hunting for nuggets of information to feed into the media machine. That meant she and the DI could have their lunch in peace and quiet and wouldn't have to deal with having a microphone shoved in their faces.

Brand brought their soft drinks over to the table a couple of minutes later and sat down across from her.

"What do you make of it all?" he said before taking a sip of his Coke.

"If we can find Mr Barker, we might glean some information about what happened at the river that day. It sounds like the boys spent a lot of time there."

"It does. The barn Diane Summers mentioned sounds like something we should have a look at as well. Isolated. Near the river. It would be perfect for Michael, if he's hiding."

"Do you think he *is* hiding?"

"I hope he is," he said, looking into his glass. "The other possibilities are less appealing."

"But more likely."

Brand nodded and took another drink. The waitress came over with the shepherd's pies and set them on the table, along with knives and forks and a small wicker basket of condiments.

When she was gone, Brand leaned forward and spoke in a lower tone. "Yes, the other possibilities are less likely, but we've got them covered. The Underwater Recovery Team is back out on the water today. If Michael is in the river, they'll find him. It might take some time due to currents and weather conditions, but they'll find him eventually if he's down there. And if he's been taken, you and I are taking the best action to cover that possibility. Speaking to the locals. Building a picture of the day's events. If he's been abducted, we'll find out."

Kate wasn't sure if he was as confident as he sounded or if he was exaggerating his assuredness that they'd solve this case just to inspire confidence in *her*. Either way, he got another positive tick on her mental tally sheet.

"Charlie seems like a nice lad," she said, taking a bite of the shepherd's pie. The mince and carrots were cooked to perfection, and the potato topping was crispy but not overcooked. She'd have to eat here more often.

"He is," the DI agreed. "It's just a shame he can't tell us more. "

"He probably knows all sorts of things if he spends his time wandering around. Probably doesn't realise what's relevant to this case. And the worse thing is, I don't think he knows that one of his friends is dead and the other is missing."

"Perhaps his parents will break the news to him."

"I doubt it. His mother seems overprotective. Perhaps with good reason based on how his father behaves."

"She can't be that overprotective. She lets him go wandering around on his own."

"Well, he is a grown adult, so she can hardly stop him. Besides, maybe she doesn't know. He might tell her he's going over to the Brady farm to see the kittens and then takes a few detours on the way home. Goes walking by the river, or whatever. His mother would never know, and his father probably doesn't care."

"True. I don't think Peggy Jones or Claire Roberts knew their boys went to the river, either. They seemed to think they were riding on the hiking trails near their homes."

"Something attracted them to the area near Stone Peak." Kate took another bite of the pie and mulled it over. "The mystery."

Brand raised an eyebrow. "You think they were trying to solve a real mystery?"

"Don't you?"

"I think it was all in their imagination. A game they were playing."

"Well, whatever it was, it kept bringing them back to the Peak."

The DI nodded sombrely.

"What about the necklace buried on the hillside?" Kate asked. "Do you think it's connected to any of this?"

"If there's a connection, I can't imagine what it might be. I've thought about that necklace a lot since the lab sent the photo, but I'm have trouble tying it to Michael and Sam. It could have nothing to do with the case at all and we just happened to stumble across it."

"Still seems odd." She finished her pie and pushed the plate away. "Why would someone bury a necklace on the Peak?"

He shrugged. "If there's one thing I've learned from years of policing, it's that people do all sorts of things for reasons known only to themselves."

She finished her drink. "That's true."

Brand's phone buzzed. He checked it and pursed his lips. Then he lowered his voice and leaned forward. "The pathologist's report on Sam Jones lists the cause of death as forcible drowning. There are bruises on Sam's chest, neck and back that suggest he was held underwater. There are also abrasion marks around his neck from his T-shirt."

Kate took a breath. The air around her felt suddenly too thick, too heavy. The confirmation that foul play had been involved meant a murderer walked among the hills and valleys of this area. That person unknown had stolen Sam's life.

The revelation also meant that the chances of Michael Roberts being found alive were much bleaker.

The DI put his phone away and stood up. "Right. Let's get back to it. We'll have a word with Henry and Lois Farrow, then pay a visit to Peggy and Claire and let them know we're doing all we can to find Michael and bring justice for Sam. The Family Liaison Officer will have broken the news to them, I expect, so it won't be an easy conversation."

As they left the pub, a drizzle of rain began to fall, darkening the landscape. Before she got into the car, Kate turned her attention to Stone Peak in the distance. Mist coiled around the summit like an ethereal wreath.

CHAPTER
FOURTEEN

THE FARROW RESIDENCE was not easily accessible. Tom swore at the Satnav as it brought them to a metal gate, beyond which a footpath skirted the boundary between a field and some woods.

"This can't be the way."

"It might be." Ryan seemed calm. She'd barely said a word since they'd left the pub, and Tom surmised that she was either still taking in the news of Sam Jones' murder or she was working on pieces of the case in her head.

His own reaction to the pathologist's report hadn't been so composed. Three times he'd cursed the "bloody roads" when the car had hit a pothole on the way here, and now this gate and path which offered no vehicular access seemed, to him, a personal affront. He gripped the steering wheel so hard his knuckles hurt.

"The Farrows must have a car," he said. "Living out

here, they need a vehicle. How do they get groceries if the only way to their house is a bloody footpath?"

"There are lots of places like this," the DS said. "People who live in them find a way to live their lives in as normal a fashion as possible." She consulted the paper map and pointed out the Farrow residence. "Look, we're here and the footpath leads to the house but there's also another path that leads there from the opposite direction. See that church car park? That's probably where the Farrows park their car. They walk to the house from there. If they have something like heavy shopping, they most likely have a quad bike to ferry stuff to and from the house."

"Sounds unnecessarily complicated to me," Tom said gruffly. He knew the pathologist's report had put him in a dark mood, but he couldn't shake it any more than he could stop the rain that was now pelting down onto the windscreen.

"Looks like the heavens have opened again," Ryan said, stepping out of the car and quickly putting her coat on.

Tom got out and went to the boot to retrieve his own coat. By the time he had it on, and had pulled the hood up, he already felt cold water seeping through his jumper. Perfect. Why not add discomfort to an already miserable day?

They set off along the footpath. Stone Peak was close, looming up on their left, beyond the trees, wreathed in mist. Tom had already surmised from the map that the Farrows lived in the shadow of the Peak.

That probably made the weather conditions worse around their house than in outlying areas. Imagine living in the middle of nowhere, in a place where it probably rained or was misty every day, and your car was parked half a mile away. He couldn't think of anything worse.

He remembered his flat in London fondly. He'd had everything he'd needed there. A chicken and kebab shop just a few yards away, a supermarket close by, and access to the rest of London via the Tube. The city seemed like a far-off fantasy world now, as he trudged along the wet footpath with the smell of cow manure assaulting his nostrils.

DS Ryan seemed to be in her element. She marched along the footpath, splashing through the puddles Tom avoided. She was probably used to the smells of the countryside. Probably didn't even notice them.

The path changed direction, leading them through the trees, approaching the Peak. Tom guessed that the area in front of him in the distance, at the base of the imposing hill, was the place where the search party was currently looking for Michael. The river was out of sight, hidden by the curve of the Peak to the east.

At last, they came upon a house. It was a simple dwelling, sitting in a clearing. A two storey, stone-built structure with a wooden porch and a smaller building that served as a garage. Ryan had been right; the garage housed a red quad bike.

Flowerpots adorned the porch, but the climbing roses that had once grown out of them were now dead.

Dry, brown stalks twisted up the walls of the house, topped with withered flowers. A kitchen chair sat on the porch next to a small wooden table upon which sat a radio which was currently silent.

As Tom and Ryan approached the porch, the door opened and a wiry man in a loose-fitting dark blue jumper and grey work trousers appeared. His white hair was shaved close to his skull, and he wore a short, white beard. Tim guessed the man's age to be early sixties, but he looked sprightly. His deep blue eyes were full of life.

"How do," the man said.

Tom hadn't heard that archaic greeting since his grandmother had passed away. "Mr Farrow? Henry Farrow?"

"That's me. And you are?"

"Detective Inspector Brand. This is Detective Sergeant Ryan. I was wondering if we could talk to you and your wife. I don't know if you're aware, but a boy has gone missing from the area. We're looking for witnesses who might have—"

"Missing?" Farrow frowned. "I don't know anything about any missing boy."

"Still, if we could talk to you and your wife."

"My wife isn't here. She's been gone over a year now. Ran away with another man. If you can find her, wherever she is, you're welcome to speak to her all you want."

"Sorry," Tom said. "I didn't realise."

Farrow shrugged the words away. "It doesn't matter

now. If she wants to go gallivanting around the world with her fancy man, that's up to her. I'm doing all right here on my own. She needn't come back here, knocking on my door when she's fed up with the high life."

Tom thought that unlikely. Farrow was probably in denial of the reality of the situation, but if that was what it took to get him through the day, he was welcome to his delusional belief. Living here alone, in the middle of nowhere, had probably affected the man in ways Tom couldn't even fathom.

"So, have you seen this boy at all?" He showed Farrow the photo of Sam and Michael by the river.

"Which one's missing? Not that it matters, I haven't seen either of them. In trouble, are they?"

"Why do you say that?"

"That's why young lads run away, isn't it? Ran away a couple of times myself when I was young, usually to avoid my father's wrath. But I always went back home eventually. I thought —wrongly, as it turned out— that he'd have cooled his heels after a week or two, but he was even angrier with me, because I'd run away. There are some situations you just can't win, I suppose."

"Right," Tom said, reaching into his coat for one of his business cards. "Well, if you do see anything…" He handed Farrow the card.

"…I'll be sure to let you know." Farrow finished for him. He reached into his pocket and pulled out a tobacco tin. He opened it and removed a hand-rolled cigarette, which he stuck between his lips and lit with a match.

Shaking the match to extinguish the flame, he said, "Is there anything else, Inspector?"

Tom knew enough about body language to realise that Farrow's was saying, *Because if there isn't, get off my land.*

"No, that's all for now," he said. "We'll be back if we have any further questions." He wasn't going to let Farrow dismiss them so easily without some sort of retort. It might be petty, but he was in a mood for pettiness. A boy was dead, another missing, and all this man wanted to do was get them off his property so he could get on with his day.

Tom and Kate headed for the footpath that had brought them here, but Tom stopped and turned, looking at Farrow, who was now leaning against the porch, watching them leave.

"Just one more thing," Tom said. He hadn't meant to sound like Columbo, and cringed inwardly when he realised he'd stolen the TV detective's catchphrase, but he continued, unable to take back the words. "Where were you on Sunday evening?"

Farrow took a drag on the cigarette and blew a cloud of smoke into the air between them. "I was here, of course. Watching television, most likely."

"What were you watching?"

The old man thought for a moment. "I don't get any channels out here, so I watch DVDs. Let's see. Sunday evening. I was watching *Rear Window*. Grace Kelly and James Stewart. Have you seen it, Detective? One of Hitchcock's best films."

"I've seen it. Like I said, we'll be in touch of there's anything further." Tom turned away, and he and Ryan left the clearing.

"Just one more thing, guv?" Ryan said when they were out of earshot. "You pulled the old Columbo trick on him."

"I wanted him to know he couldn't just dismiss us like that. This is a murder investigation." He took a deep breath and let it out slowly to calm himself down. "Apart from his rudeness, what did you think of him?"

"He probably didn't even know he was being rude. He lives out here on his own for a reason; he doesn't like people. He's not bothered about social graces. I don't think it was personal. As for whether or not he's connected to the case, I doubt it. He probably *was* sitting in front of the telly all evening. That's probably his life."

Grudgingly, Tom agreed. And if he was honest with himself, he'd met a thousand people in the course of his career who were a thousand times ruder than Henry Farrow had just been. He was overreacting because of the circumstances of the day. Not only had Sam Jones been proven to be the victim of a killer, but Tom also had to face Michael Roberts' parents with no news to tell them regarding their son's whereabouts.

They were going out of their minds with worry, and he had uncovered nothing to reunite them with Michael. He couldn't even bring them closure.

CHAPTER
FIFTEEN

KATE STEELED herself for the meeting with Michael Roberts' parents. She and Brand waited in the car outside the Roberts residence, the rain bouncing off the car roof and running down the windows in rivulets, blurring the world outside.

"I've asked the Family Liaison Officer to meet us out here before we go in," Brand said. "I want to know how much the Roberts have been told before we speak to them. We don't want to blunder in there and upset anybody more than we have to."

The front door opened, and a middle-aged black woman dressed in a dark blue skirt and white blouse came outside, holding an umbrella over her head as she made her way to the car. She gave them a wave and opened the rear door, slipping into the backseat as she collapsed the umbrella.

"Hiya," she said, shutting the rain out. "I'm Dina Prince, the FLO working with the Roberts family."

"DI Tom Brand." He reached back to shake her hand.

"DS Kate Ryan," Kate said, doing the same.

"Everyone is very upset, as you can imagine," Dina said. "I broke the news to them about the pathologist's report earlier and it didn't go well. They realise that the verdict on Sam's death means it's less likely Michael is going to come home unharmed. They still have a thread of hope, of course, but it's wearing thin with every bit of bad news."

"Quite understandable," Brand said. "Is Peggy Jones still in the house with them?"

"She's gone home. Her mother is with her, and so is my colleague, Trish Bates. Needless to say, Peggy is distraught."

Brand nodded. "Of course."

"Are we any closer to finding out what happened to Michael?" Dina asked.

Brand let out a sigh. "Not yet, I'm afraid. We've got a few leads to track down but there's nothing solid."

"So, you don't have anything positive to tell them?"

"No." Brand's face was grim.

"Then this will be a rough conversation. Claire is in bits and her husband, John, is full of anger. He wants to know why his son hasn't been found yet."

"We're doing all we can."

"I know." Dina leaned forward and spoke softly. "But you need to tell *them* that."

Brand nodded and got out of the car. Ignoring the

rain, he walked to the front door and pushed it open, going inside. Dina and Kate followed.

Kate hated discussions with families who had lost loved ones. If there was something to tell them, some news to convey, that was one thing; but informing them that you weren't any closer to finding their loved one was heartbreaking.

She followed Brand into the living room, where Claire Roberts sat on a sofa, clutching a baby to her chest, while her husband stood facing the DI.

"Where is my son? You've been out there for two days. He can't have just vanished."

"It isn't that simple, sir," Brand said.

"Of course it's that simple. Michael is out there somewhere, and you can't find him. How much taxpayers' money have you wasted wandering around the countryside for two days, getting nowhere?"

The baby started to cry. Claire Roberts shot her husband a frustrated look and left the room. Kate heard her footsteps on the stairs.

"I don't know why you bothered coming here if you've got nothing to tell us," John Roberts continued. "You should be out there looking for my boy instead of standing in my living room. He's not here, is he? He's out there. In the rain. In the cold."

He collapsed onto the sofa his wife had just vacated, a look of despair filling his eyes. "He's not here," he repeated, softly this time. Burying his face in his hands, he began to weep.

Dina moved to the DI and put a hand on his shoulder, gently guiding him back to the living room door.

"I'll handle it from here," she whispered. "You two should probably go."

Brand nodded in agreement and left the house, striding out into the rain. Kate wasn't sure if he was angry or upset, but there was definitely some sort of emotion bubbling beneath the surface.

"Sorry," she whispered to Dina. "We've made things worse."

"You have nothing to apologise for; it's just how things are."

Kate nodded and left the house. When she got into the car, the DI was staring through the rain-streaked windscreen, and now Kate could see that the emotion he was trying to control was anger. His jaw was set, the muscles in his cheeks contracting and releasing. His eyes were fixed on the blurry road in front of the car, his hands gripping the steering wheel like claws, as if he were trying to navigate a narrow road full of twists and turns, even though the car wasn't moving.

She knew he wasn't angry at John Roberts. Brand was much too professional for that. His anger was directed at the situation. Two days of searching had produced nothing. Michael Roberts was still missing — or dead, which she knew the DI was accepting as the most likely outcome as each day passed, just as she was — and they were getting nowhere.

She sat in silence, waiting for him to deal with his

emotions in whatever way he could. Like most detectives she knew, Brand would have some sort of coping mechanism. Her own was to think of her mother. The mystery surrounding her death —or at least what Kate considered a mystery, even though nobody else seemed to— had enough threads to pick at that doing so usually made Kate overcome her current mental state as she worked on a puzzle that seemed impossible to solve.

Gradually, Brand's grip on the wheel loosened and his jaw relaxed. He looked over at Kate and said, "Right, let's go and see Peggy Jones."

CHAPTER
SIXTEEN

PEGGY JONES' house was only a few streets away from the Roberts' residence, and Kate could see why Michael and Sam were allowed to ride to each other's homes without their parents being concerned.

She estimated the distance from here to the Stone Peak trail to be no more than half a mile. The boys could cover that distance in three or four minutes easily on their bicycles. While they were spending time on the trail by the river, they were believed to be safe, riding around the streets close to home, or perhaps even at each other's houses.

Michael and Sam had been roaming the wilderness, and their parents had been none the wiser.

Peggy's house looked like a carbon copy of the Roberts residence except for a planter full of climbing roses under the living room window. The roses were young and hadn't made much progress up the wall. Kate wondered if Sam had helped his mother plant them earlier in the year. Had the two of them spent time together out here, planting the young roses in the soil, both unaware that Sam would not be around to see them grow?

They got out of the car and walked up the short path to the front door. The DI knocked gently, as if trying not to disturb anyone in the house any more than he had to.

The door opened and a woman in her fifties stuck her head through the gap. Her face was set into an expression of wariness and anger combined. "We're not talking to the press." She began to close the door.

"We're the police," Brand said, taking out his warrant card and showing it to her through the narrowing gap in the doorway. "Is Peggy home?"

The woman, still wary, nodded and opened the door wider. Brand and Kate slipped inside, and the door was closed quickly behind them.

"I'm Claudia," the woman said. "Peggy's mother. She's upstairs, in Sam's room. Crying, of course. She's been crying all day. I don't know what to do with her. That boy was the light of her life, and now he's gone. What can you say to make that better?" She wiped a tear from her cheek.

A younger, fair-haired woman appeared from the kitchen at the back of the house. "Come on, Claudia, I've made you a cup of tea." Turning her attention to Kate and the DI, she said, "Trish Bates, Family Liaison Officer."

Everyone introduced themselves and the FLO led

them to the kitchen. Claudia sat down heavily at the table, her expression one of grief as she sipped her tea.

"Obviously, this hasn't been a good day," Trish said, refilling the kettle. "Peggy has been in Sam's room for the last hour. We're giving her time to come to terms with the recent developments.

"Her son was killed," Claudia said, still staring into her tea. "How could she ever come to terms with that? How could anybody?"

Trish opened a cupboard and placed three mugs on the counter. "Would you like a cup of tea, Detectives?"

The DI nodded but Kate refused. "I'd like to talk to Peggy, if that's all right."

"I'll come with you," Brand said.

"No, you stay here and have a cuppa. It might be better if I go on my own." She was sure the DI could be diplomatic and sympathetic, but the sight of the two of them might overwhelm Peggy.

He nodded his assent and sat down at the table.

"It's the first room on the left," Trish said.

Kate took a deep breath and made her way to the foot of the stairs, her mind racing with what she was going to say to the woman who was grieving in her dead son's room.

If she hated these conversations so much, why had she volunteered to do this? She knew the answer as soon as she asked herself the question. She saw a kindred spirit in Peggy Jones. Both she and Peggy had lost a loved one and neither of them had any answers that could penetrate the veil of mystery surrounding that loss.

She ascended the stairs slowly, past framed pictures of Peggy and Sam that hung on the walls. In some of the pictures, which showed smiling faces and happier times, a dark-haired man also smiled at the camera. Kate knew that Peggy's husband, David, had passed away some years ago.

When she reached the landing, she turned left and came face to face with a white, wooden door and the word's *Sam's Room* on a metal plaque in the style of an American license plate.

Clearing her throat self-consciously, knowing she was about to intrude on a private moment in Peggy's life, Kate knocked softly on the door.

There was a moment of silence, during which Kate almost turned around and went back downstairs, and then a woman's voice said weakly, "Come in."

Kate opened the door and stuck her head inside the room. What she saw took her by surprise. Peggy Jones was sitting on the bed, surrounded by open board games, whose contents had been scattered across the sheets and the floor, and paperback books which had been opened and strewn all over the room. A wardrobe stood open and all of Sam's clothes which contained pockets —jackets, trousers, and jeans— had been spread over the floor, the pockets turned inside out.

Kate had been into the bedrooms of lost children before, and usually the state of those bedrooms had been the opposite to what she saw in front of her. They were immaculately preserved, every toy and article of clothing in its place. Shrines to a memory.

Sam's room had been dismantled piece by piece.

"I was just trying to find something that would tell me why," Peggy said. "Something I must have missed. Something I should have known." She threw her hands up at the mess surrounding her. "But there's nothing."

"Would you like me to help you tidy up?" Kate offered.

Peggy nodded, wiping tears from her eyes.

Kate started by picking up the scattered books and placing them into a bookcase that sat beneath the window. Some of the books were familiar from her own childhood. *Sherlock Holmes*, *The Famous Five*, *The Secret Seven*, *Nancy Drew*, *The Hardy Boys*, and *The Three Investigators*. "I'm Kate, by the way. I'm a detective working on your son's case." She picked up a copy of *The Return of Sherlock Holmes* and placed it on the shelf.

"Have you found Michael yet?" Peggy asked.

"No, not yet."

"Poor Claire and John. They must be going out of their minds with worry."

Kate tightened her lips and focused on the task of tidying up. This woman had just lost her son and she still had enough empathy left to worry about her friends.

"Peggy, I'm here to let you know that we're doing all we can to find out exactly what happened to your son. We won't give up until someone is brought to justice."

"Thank you."

When the books were in the bookcase, as neatly as Kate could arrange them, she turned her attention to the clothes, folding them and placing them into the wardrobe.

Peggy moved from the bed, collecting the open board game boxes together and gathering dice, playing pieces, and cards from the floor. She placed everything on the bed in one big pile. Regarding the chaos of cardboard and plastic with a look of helplessness, she said, "I don't know how I'm ever going to put these back in the right boxes."

Kate closed the wardrobe door. "I'll help. We'll do the best we can."

Together, they tried to match the various playing pieces with the correct boxes. Kate picked up a double-faced playing card that had the two of hearts on one side, and the jack of clubs on the reverse. "Where does this go?" she asked Peggy.

"The magic set. I bought it for Sam's ninth birthday." She sighed. "He was never really interested in it. It's been sitting in the back of his wardrobe ever since."

Kate spied a box that had a picture of a top hat and a rabbit on it and the words *You Can Do Magic!* She opened it and placed the double-faced card inside, next to a set of interlinked metal rings, a selection of other playing cards, and a red velvet cloth with a yellow trim.

She closed the box and gathered up a pile of Monopoly playing pieces before remembering the ragged piece of red velvet and the necklace that had been buried on Stone Peak.

She reopened the magic set and pulled out the red fabric, unfolding it and laying it flat on the bed.

A ragged square had been cut out of the centre.

Peggy narrowed her eyes at the hole. "Well, I knew he wasn't keen on it, but I didn't know he'd done that. Must have been part of some trick or other."

Kate kept her emotions in check, realising she had found a piece of evidence in the case. She refolded the fabric and said, "I'm going to need to take this with me."

CHAPTER
SEVENTEEN

"SO, it *was* the boys who buried that necklace on the Peak," Tom said. They were sitting in his car outside the Jones residence, the velvet cloth in a clear evidence bag on the dashboard. It would go to the lab to be compared against the fabric found inside the Tupperware container, but it was obvious that this was the same material the necklace had been wrapped in.

"Looks like it." Ryan had been in a contemplative mood since talking to Peggy Jones, simply informing him that they should leave the house and then, in the car, revealing the velvet cloth.

"And this was in Sam's magic set?"

"Peggy said Sam didn't like it. It's been at the back of his wardrobe for years."

"But he found a use for it when he wanted to bury the necklace. The question is: why? Why did they bury the necklace in the first place? Where did they get it from?"

"It wasn't Peggy's. I asked her if she owned a necklace with a pendant shaped like the sun and she said she didn't. She also told me she doesn't own any Tupperware."

He picked up his phone. "I'm going to send the picture of the necklace to Dina Prince and ask her if the Roberts family recognises it. I'll mention the Tupperware."

Tom found Dina's number. He sent her the photo, along with a message that simply said, *Do the Roberts own any Tupperware and is any missing?*

"I really didn't think the necklace was connected to the boys," Ryan said. "I didn't see how it could be."

"I'm racking my brains trying to see a connection myself," he admitted.

"Perhaps they stole it," Ryan said. "And the person they stole it from is the person who killed Sam."

"It's possible, but from what we know about the boys it seems unlikely."

She nodded in agreement. They had no reason to believe the boys were thieves.

Yet the necklace had been secreted away for a reason.

Tom's phone rang. It was Dina.

"Claire doesn't recognise the necklace," she said. "But she checked her Tupperware set and the smallest container is missing. They're asking questions; what shall I tell them?"

"I don't know," Tom said truthfully, "because I don't know what any of it means myself yet."

"Okay. Well, as soon as you have anything to pass on, you know my number." She hung up.

"It looks like the Tupperware came from Claire Roberts' kitchen," Tom told Ryan. "So, Michael and Sam got the necklace from somewhere and then went to the trouble of acquiring the velvet to wrap it in and the container to protect it before burying it on Stone Peak."

"It doesn't make any sense," she said.

Tom checked his watch. The search team would be packing up right about now. It was too late to join them. And the fact that they hadn't been in contact meant they'd been unsuccessful in locating Michael.

"I suggest we call it a day," he said. "The new support team starts at the station tomorrow. They can find Mr Barker. If they get a hit, we can conduct an interview."

"Sounds like a plan."

"There's something else we need to do as well. I want to have a look at that barn Diane Brady mentioned. The isolated one on George Gibbon's farm." He couldn't think of a better place for Michael Roberts to be hiding, or —if he had been abducted— to be held captive.

When Tom got back to his father's house, the rain had slowed to an intermittent drizzle. The sun had dropped beneath the horizon, but its light still partially illuminated the atmosphere. Tom found his dad in the greenhouse, picking tomatoes in the twilight and placing them into a wicker basket. The old man was completely absorbed by the task and didn't notice his son watching him through the greenhouse glass.

Beyond the greenhouse, vegetable plots had been dug and labelled. Canes and netting rose from some of the plots, bean and pea vines twisting around them. In others, hordes of green leaves spread over the soil, promising a bountiful harvest of carrots and potatoes beneath.

In the distance, dark silhouettes of hills rolled beneath the twilight sky.

Watching his father pottering around in the greenhouse while humming happily to himself, Tom wondered how he was going to convince this man to move from the place he loved so much and relocate to the city. Replacing the expansive garden of vegetable plots with a window box on the balcony of a London flat, and the distant, rolling hills with tall, geometric tower blocks would crush his father's spirit.

"Tom, I didn't see you there. Everything all right?"

"Everything's fine," Tom said, entering the greenhouse. The smell of tomato plants hung in the air, as well as a hint of his dad's cedar wood aftershave.

"Let me help you with that." Tom picked up the basket and carried it out of the greenhouse.

His father followed closely behind. "How was your day?"

"It didn't go as well as I would have liked, but we've made some progress."

"Excellent! It's still early days. I'm sure you'll break the case, given a bit more time."

They entered the house through the back door and went into the kitchen. Tom put the basket of tomatoes on the counter. "Any particular reason you picked these tonight?"

"I was hoping we could have some more of your homemade pasta sauce. It was lovely."

"Of course." Tom didn't mind cooking. He knew that after a day in the garden, his father would be tired and aching. He set about preparing the meal.

His dad took a seat at the table and said, "Kate not joining us tonight?"

"No, DS Ryan will not be joining us tonight. That was a one-off situation."

"That's a shame. I like her. You do, too."

"She's a proficient detective," Tom said.

"Proficient?"

"All right, very proficient."

"I'm not talking about her professional skills, Tom. I mean her personality."

"Oh. Yes." Tom concentrated on chopping the tomatoes.

Seeming to sense Tom's reluctance to talk about the matter, his dad said, "I'm glad you've made some progress on the case."

"Actually, Dad, there's something I was going to ask you. What do you know about George Gibbon?"

His father chuckled. "Ah, you've tangled with George, have you?"

"I haven't, but he ran DS Ryan and one of the constables off his farm."

"That sounds about right. George has always been a grumpy so-and-so. He and his neighbour had a bit of a feud back in the day when they both tried to court Wendy Stiles. George ended up marrying her, so you'd think he'd be happy, but married life doesn't seem to have improved his demeanour any."

"You mean his neighbour Wesley Brady?"

"Yes, Wesley. There's no love lost between those two, even today, thirty-odd years later."

"Surely they aren't still feuding over Wendy. Wesley is with Diane now."

"They've only been together for three or four years. Before that, Wesley was married to a woman named Catherine. Unhappily, by all accounts."

"What happened to her?" Tom asked, placing a cup of pasta into a pan of boiling water. His father's local knowledge could prove invaluable where the suspects in this case were concerned. Not that George Gibbon was a suspect, but Tom wasn't discounting anyone at this point.

"She and Wesley never really got on. She left eventually. They'd always be arguing in the Mermaid, or in the village. There were a couple of domestic disturbance calls to the police as well, as I recall. Wesley spent at least one night in a cell because his arguments with Catherine had progressed past slinging insults at each other and had become physical altercations."

He frowned, as if trying to remember something. "I can't recall exactly when she left. Maybe ten years ago. She just stopped showing up at the pub and after a while, Wesley told everyone she'd packed her bags and done a runner in the middle of the night."

"Perhaps that was the only way she could get away," Tom suggested.

His dad shrugged. "Yes, I suppose it might have been. Anyway, as you said, Wesley is with Diane now, and he seems much happier for it. I'm sure that as far as he's concerned, his feud with George Gibbon is a thing of the past."

Tom reflected on that while the pasta cooked. He had to be careful not to become distracted by an old neighbourly dispute, but it was something worth keeping in the back of his mind.

When the pasta was ready, he drained the pan over the sink before dividing the pasta between two dishes and adding the savoury sauce. He took the meals over to the table and sat down. "Do you know anything about an old barn on the Gibbon farm?"

"Yes, I think I know the one you mean. It's at the very edge of the farm, not far from the river. Falling apart, if I recall." His dad leaned forward, intrigued. "Is there a particular reason you're interested in it?"

Tom shrugged. "I think it's worth looking at. Like you say, it's close to the river. It would provide Michael Roberts with shelter and a place to hide."

"Hide from whom?"

"If I knew that, I'd have already solved the case."

His father pursed his lips. "You don't really think Michael is hiding somewhere, do you?"

"Until we know otherwise, I'm going to assume he's still alive."

"I suppose the barn is worth checking out, in any case."

"Yes, that's what I was thinking."

They ate in silence for a few minutes until his father said, "This pasta is delicious."

Tom, who had been thinking of the river and wondering how long a body could stay hidden in its murky depths, replied, "It's the fresh tomatoes from your greenhouse that make all the difference."

And with that, the subject was changed.

CHAPTER
EIGHTEEN

KATE SAT in her car staring at the landscape. She had driven out of Relby and parked by the side of a road that wound up a high pass. The panoramic view of rolling hills stretching to the horizon might soothe the soul of any nature lover, but for Kate, the scene was bittersweet.

Kinder Scout rose from the distant moorland, its peak touching the low, sun-tinged clouds. This was the place where her mother's body had been discovered twenty-five years ago, exposed on the hillside near the summit.

Kate had seen this view often during her lifetime. She frequently parked her car here, on this high pass, in this exact spot, and pondered the immense hill —the highest point in the Peak District— wondering what had happened there all those years ago. Why had her mother ascended the hill during one of the worst storms in decades?

When she was sixteen, ten years to the day after her mother's death, Kate had climbed Kinder Scout herself, thinking she might feel closer to her mother by being in the place where the woman had perished. But she had felt nothing except loneliness. She'd returned home in a flood of tears, grieving what might have been if her mother had survived. A piece of herself was missing; a piece she could never truly know.

From that day forward, she had dreamed about her mother every night.

The phone rattled on the dashboard, startling her out of her thoughts. She answered it quickly, hoping it was the DI calling with an update on the case. "DS Ryan."

"Kate, it's your aunt. No need to sound so formal."

"Aunt Justine. How are you?"

"I'm a little bit disappointed, dear, to be honest."

"Disappointed?" Kate had no idea what her aunt was referring to.

"Yes, disappointed, dear. We were watching a news report this morning about a murder in Relby. Your Uncle Gary pointed at the TV and said, "That's our Kate!" Well, at first, I thought he was mistaken, and it must have been someone who looked like you. I mean, you're working in Matlock, not Relby...or so I thought. But then the camera panned around and there you were, standing outside the house next door to the murder victim. And I said to Gary, "You're right, that *is* our Kate!"

Kate groaned inwardly. She knew exactly where this conversation was heading.

"So, your Uncle Gary and I were wondering why — if you're working on a case so close to home— you haven't rung us. Where are you staying, love? I know it isn't with your dad, because I rang him, and he had no idea you were here either."

"I'm staying at a B&B in the village. I need to be close to the police station."

"We're only a twenty-minute drive from Relby, love, and your dad is no more than half an hour away. Come and stay with us; you don't want to be cooped up in a B&B when your family's so close. We've got plenty of room here, and we'd love to see you."

Kate sighed with resignation. There was no way she was going to get out of this. Her Aunt Justine was a persistent woman and wouldn't see a family member 'slumming it' in a B&B when there was a perfectly good spare bed at her house.

And what was wrong with that? Why *hadn't* Kate called them when she knew she was going to be working in Relby? Too busy to get around to it, she told herself. But was that really the reason? How long had it been it since she had seen Aunt Justine and Uncle Gary? Or her own dad, for that matter?

"All right, I'll come and see you tomorrow," she said.

"Are you busy tonight or something?" Aunt Justine asked. "Working late?"

"No, I'm just…" Kate looked at the imposing peak

of Kinder Scout in the distance, "...appreciating the landscape."

"Well, get yourself over here now, dear. I've got a cottage pie in the oven, with new potatoes, garden peas, and Yorkshire puddings to go with it. You love Yorkies and new potatoes."

The offer made Kate's mouth water. Her aunt was a magnificent cook, and Kate hadn't eaten a decent meal since the spaghetti she'd had at the DI's house yesterday. "All right, I'll be there in about an hour."

"Bring your suitcase with you. We've got plenty of room now that Millie and Sarah have moved out. You can stay as long as you like, and I won't take no for an answer." Aunt Justine hung up.

Kate placed the phone back on the dashboard, smiling as she did so. It looked like she'd be staying with her aunt and uncle for the remainder of this case. It beat staying at the B&B hands down, and she hadn't seen them in so long, it would be good to catch up.

The phone rang again. This time, she checked the screen before answering. *DCI Holt*. Kate groaned as she picked up the device.

"Hello, ma'am."

"Ryan, what have you got to report?"

"Nothing much, ma'am. I'm sure you've read the official reports. The cloth used to wrap the necklace was from Sam Jones' house, and—"

"Yes, yes, I know all that. I mean who are your suspects? Who are you interviewing?"

"It's all in the reports."

DCI Holt made a noise that was somewhere between a sigh and a frustrated growl that rose from the back of her throat.

Kate wasn't sure what she was supposed to say. Everything she and DI Brand had done —everyone they'd interviewed— had been carefully documented.

"I'm not talking about the official line, Detective Sergeant. What are you and Brand talking about behind the scenes?"

"Behind the scenes, ma'am?"

"You know what I mean. Conversations on the way to and from crime scenes. Theories. Ideas. Pieces of information the locals have mentioned that you haven't put in the report."

"There's nothing like that, ma'am." Why was the DCI fishing for information? Wasn't she satisfied with how the investigation was going? Kate was frustrated too —especially with not knowing where Michael was — but she and Brand were doing the best they could.

"Well, let's see," the DCI said, seemingly undeterred, "What's your impression of…Wesley Brady, for example? Has he mentioned anything that you didn't think worthy of recording?"

The DCI tried to make the comment seem casual, as if she'd chosen Wesley's name randomly, but Kate wasn't fooled; she knew when someone was trying to sound too offhand.

"It's all in the reports, ma'am," she said flatly.

Holt paused, perhaps realising she'd been rumbled. Her voice became officious. "Right. Well, keep me informed if there are any developments." She ended the call.

Kate stared at the phone for a moment before placing it on the dashboard. What the hell was going on? Why was the DCI so interested in Wesley Brady? She closed her eyes and tried to recall the conversation with Wesley, attempting to pinpoint something — anything— that could be of interest to the DCI.

She couldn't remember anything out of the ordinary, but then she had no idea what information Holt was referring to. Why did Holt want inside information on what the local residents were talking about? Why was she trying to use the investigation to eavesdrop on Brady?

"Make it make sense," Kate whispered. She had to be missing a vital clue; something that linked the DCI and the farmer.

Should she tell Brand? She stared out at the wild, darkening landscape. Perhaps she should wait until she had something more than unfounded suspicion. She needed evidence. That meant she was going to have to carry out a clandestine investigation during her own time.

"Fine," she muttered to herself. "Then that's what I'll do."

She wasn't sure where she was going to start, but somehow or other she was going to get to the bottom of this. Holt had a secret, and now that Kate had caught a hint of it, she needed to discover what it was. If it was somehow related to this case —or to someone possibly connected to the case, like Wesley Brady— she had a duty to uncover it.

She started the car and pulled away from the side of the road, leaving the view of Kinder Scout behind and putting all thoughts of DCI Holt aside, concentrating instead on the road ahead.

An hour later, she parked the Jeep outside Aunt Justine's house, her suitcase on the back seat. Her aunt and uncle lived in a large stone house that had once been a farmhouse but now sat on a modest amount of land, the rest having been sold off by the previous resident to a construction firm that had built a housing estate whose yellow-brick, modern dwellings seemed totally out of place in the rugged landscape.

The front door opened, warm light spilling from the interior of the house and brightening the evening gloom. Aunt Justine appeared in the doorway, wiping her hands on a white apron that she wore over a russet-coloured turtleneck jumper and dark slacks.

"I've made an apple pie to welcome you home, dear," she said as Kate heaved the suitcase out of the Jeep.

"You shouldn't have," Kate said, although as she approached the house and smelled the heady mix of apple, cinnamon, and cooked pastry, she was glad Justine had.

Her aunt gave her a hug on the doorstep, pulling Kate into a warm embrace. "It's good to have you back, Kate."

"It's been too long," Kate said.

"It has. Leave your suitcase in the hall and Gary will take it up to the spare room for you." She turned to the interior of the house and shouted, "Gary, Kate's here."

Uncle Gary came out of the living room, where the television was blaring. Gary had always had bad hearing, and it seemed to have become worse since Kate had last seen him. "Kate!" he exclaimed, drawing her into a quick hug and then releasing her. "How's life in the police force?"

"Busy," she said.

"Yes, we've been following the case of those boys on the news. And now that photographer has been killed. Looks like you've got your hands full."

"She doesn't want to talk about that now," Justine said. "Take her case upstairs, Gary, it's nearly time to eat. Come on, Kate." She set off towards the kitchen at the back of the house.

Kate followed, passing a framed photograph of her mother and Justine when they were young girls. Justine, the youngest by two years, was sitting on top of a stone wall in a field of sheep. Kate's mother, who looked nine or ten-years-old in the photo, stood on the far side of the wall with only her head and hands visible as she peeked over at the camera. Both girls had wide grins on their faces.

The kitchen had retained its farmhouse feel, with a range oven, wooden cabinets, and a large porcelain sink. A large oak table dominated the space and Aunt Justine gestured for Kate to take a seat while she fussed over the Aga. The smell of baked apple pie was even more mouth-watering in here, the sweet scent mixing with the savoury smells emanating from a cottage pie that sat in a large, orange-coloured casserole dish on the wooden counter.

Justine took the apple pie out of the oven and set it to one side to cool. As she did so, the doorbell rang. "That'll be your dad, Kate. When I told him you were coming over, he asked if he could join us, so of course I said yes. It's been a while since he last saw you."

Kate tried to remember the last time she had seen her dad and realised that although she spoke to him regularly on the phone, it had been over two months since she'd actually spoken to him face to face. She'd been so busy that time had crept away unnoticed.

She went to the front door and opened it. Her dad stood outside with a big grin on his face. "Kate!" He opened his arms for a hug.

"Hi, Dad." Kate wrapped her arms tightly around him. The hug was familiar and comforting. He smelled of the aftershave she'd bought him last Christmas.

"Pies ready!" Janine called from the kitchen. "Come and get it while it's hot!"

"Something smells good," Kate's dad said, stepping

into the house. He followed Kate to the kitchen, where Uncle Gary was already seated at the head of the table.

"How do, Rob?" Gary said when he saw Kate's father. "Life treating you all right?"

"Can't complain, Gary. Did you see the match?"

Gary rolled his eyes. "Abysmal. Half the team needs to learn how to kick a ball."

Dinner was served and tasted just as delicious as its mouth-watering smell had promised. As Kate watched the friendly banter between her family members and savoured every mouthful of the cottage pie, Yorkshire puddings, and potatoes, she tried to imagine how her mother would fit into this family dynamic had she been here. Would she have laughed at Gary's jokes? Eaten an entire plate of cottage pie and asked for seconds, as Kate was considering doing? Would she sit close to her husband, sharing intimate space comfortably with him?

Kate would never know. It was at times like this, when family members shared food and conversation and closeness, that a tiny part of her resented her mother for leaving all this behind and no longer being a part of it. Then Kate would inevitably feel guilty for harbouring such an emotion. She pushed the thought of her mother's absence away and tried to concentrate on the warmth and love around the dining table in front of her.

But when the subject of the police investigation came up and her father said, "Your mother would be so proud of you, Kate," she could only offer a quick, cold smile in return.

WEDNESDAY

CHAPTER
NINETEEN

A YOUNG WOMAN with long red hair came bustling into the office on Wednesday morning, a cardboard box balanced in her arms. She was neatly dressed in a blue blouse and black skirt and her makeup had been applied immaculately, but her hair was plastered against her forehead with perspiration, her face flushed with exertion.

Tom, who had been looking out at the bright morning while drinking his first coffee of the day, started as the door slammed against the wall.

"Sorry I'm late, sir." She dropped the box onto a desk by the window. "Can I sit here? That's a wonderful view."

"Sit wherever you like." Tom checked the clock on the wall. It was five to nine. "And you're not late at all. You're five minutes early, in fact."

She looked at her watch, her eyebrows arching with surprise. "Ah, right. That's good, then."

"In fact, you're the first member of the team to arrive. I assume you are part of the support team?"

"I *am* the support team, sir. Tilly Francis."

She held out her hand. Tom shook it, as surprised by her strong grip as he was by the revelation that she was the entire support team for the station. Holt hadn't mentioned how many people would be on the team, but the word itself had implied more than one.

Tilly removed various items from the cardboard box and arranged them on the desk, populating the workstation with pens, notebooks, a pink mousepad, and a potted spider plant which she placed on the windowsill.

"When you're settled, I want you to find the address of a Mr Barker." he told her. "Probably local. Walks his dog by the river. We need to talk to him, but I don't have any more details than that, I'm afraid."

Tilly opened a notebook, found a blank page, and plucked a pen from the desk. "Mr Barker. Local. Got it."

"Let me know when you have something." Tom finished the coffee in his office, studying the weather reports. No rain today, according to the forecast. Not much wind either, except on the hills. That was fine. He didn't expect to be out on the hills today; he had a barn to inspect. Technically, he needed the owner's permission to enter the barn, but it sounded like the structure was derelict, so it probably wouldn't be locked, and might not even have a door. Besides, a child was missing. Tom had to search everywhere.

Ten minutes later, there was knock on his open office

door. Tilly came in with a scrap of paper in her hand. "I think I've found Mr Barker, sir. There's an Edward Barker who lives on Church Street. He's the only registered resident at the address. He owns a dog licence, so he's likely our man." She placed the slip of paper in front of Tom.

He looked at the address that Tilly had written in neat, swirling script. Church Street ran alongside St Paul's Church in the village. It was certainly close enough to Stone Peak for someone who lived there to take their dog for a daily walk on the trail by the river.

"If he's not the Mr Barker we're looking for, I'll search further afield," Tilly said, "but he's the most likely candidate."

"Thank you, Tilly."

She moved to the door but then paused and hovered there.

"Is there something else?" Tom asked.

"Well, yes, actually. Could you tell me where the loo is?"

Tom was about to answer when DS Ryan appeared. "I'll show her." She smiled at Tilly and said, "Come on, it's just upstairs. We've got a kitchen up there as well, and a staff breakout area."

As they went upstairs, Ryan asked, "Are you part of the support team?".

"I *am* the support team."

"Oh." Ryan sounded bewildered.

Tom grabbed his jacket and waited for the DS to return. When she came back downstairs, he held up the slip of paper. "Tilly found an address for an Edward Barker on Church Street."

"You think he's the mysterious Mr Barker?"

"He's certainly worth talking to. Then we can have a look at that barn."

They left the station and crossed the road on foot. Two minutes later, they stood outside the front door of Edward Barker's residence. The house looked virtually identical to every other house on the street. A short path led from the pavement over a small, tidy front garden to the house, which had a bay window overlooking the street. The only thing that distinguished this particular house from the others was a small hand-painted sign attached to the front door that read, *Edward Barker Photography. Weddings, Pets, Portraits.*

Tom knocked on the door. There was no reply. He knocked again, louder this time.

An upstairs window opened next door and a woman in her eighties, grey hair in rollers, poked her head out. "If you're looking for Edward, he's not in. He walks his dog every day at this time. Come back later." With that said, she retracted her head back inside and closed the window.

Tom turned to Ryan, raising an eyebrow. "Sounds like we'll find him at the river."

They retraced their steps back to the station and got into Tom's car.

As he started the car and pulled out of the car park, Tom realised that DS Ryan was unusually quiet this morning. She seemed distracted, as if she had something on her mind.

Probably the case, he told himself. He knew the feeling. He'd hardly slept last night, waking up every hour while his overactive mind tried to pick apart the mysterious threads surrounding the fate of the boys. He had finally come to the conclusion, sitting up in bed at three a.m. while silvery moonlight diffused through the curtains and crept over the sheets, that a part of the puzzle was missing.

No matter how hard he applied his mind to the problem, this case could not be solved yet. Certain elements needed to fall into place first. The missing bicycles. The notebook the boys carried around with them. The necklace buried on the hill. It all meant something, but at the moment it meant nothing.

He decided not to ask Ryan if she was okay. She had directed her gaze out of the car window to the trees at the side of the road. Probably running over the details of the case in her mind. Tom concentrated on driving. When she was ready to talk, he'd be willing to listen. Until then, he was going to focus on finding the clues that would bring the puzzle pieces together with a final *click*.

Edward Barker might know something. The photographer might not even *know* that he knew something. If he spent his time taking photos on the path that ran along the river, his camera might have caught something relevant to the case.

Don't get ahead of yourself, Tom warned himself

mentally. *Chase the clues, but don't expect them to fall into your lap. You'll only be disappointed if they don't materialise.*

The car park came into view, now open to the public again. A handful of cars were parked in the area, but no news vans, thankfully. Tom found a space and killed the engine.

"How are we going to recognise Barker, guv?" Ryan asked as she got out of the car.

"Easy," he said. "We look for a man with a dog and a camera."

The first thing he noticed when he stepped onto the trail was the absence of the Underwater Recover Team on the river. Surely they hadn't stopped looking, had they? He was reaching for his phone, ready to chase up the matter when he spotted the dinghy a quarter of a mile downriver. They'd covered a lot of water since beginning their search.

But still no sign of Michael. Maybe he isn't in the river after all.

"Perhaps Michael isn't down there," Ryan said, obviously thinking the same thing. She paused and then added, "Maybe we'll find him alive."

Tom mentally repeated the warning he'd given himself earlier about not expecting anything that might never materialise. But he wasn't willing to totally discount the slim chance of Michael being alive, so he simply said, "We'll see," and continued along the path in search of Edward Barker.

A black and white dog came barrelling toward them, tail wagging as it hurled itself along the trail. Then a male voice shouted, "Fred, get back here!" and the dog stopped immediately. It huffed and turned tail, loping back the way it had come.

The man who had called the dog stood at the river's edge, not far from the spot where the bike markings had been found in the mud. The man's hands were buried in the pockets of an olive-green windbreaker. A tripod stood on the ground next to him. A camera fixed on top of the tripod pointed at the river.

"Mr Edward Barker?" Tom asked as he got closer to the man.

"Yes, that's me. How can I help?" Barker was in his 50s, balding, and short with a stocky build.

"Detective Inspector Brand," Tom said. "And this is Detective Sergeant Ryan. We'd like to ask you a couple of questions."

The photographer raised a quizzical eyebrow. "All right, ask away."

"We understand you spend quite a lot of time in this area."

"Well, I walk my dog here every day, if that's what you mean."

"Did you know the two boys who went missing here recently?"

"I wouldn't say I knew them. Saw them riding their bikes on the trail a few times. Spoke to them a couple of times in passing. Took some photos of them when they were climbing up the hillside." His brow furrowed and he sighed. "Damn shame what happened to them."

"We're not sure what happened to Michael yet," Tom reminded him.

"No, of course not, but it isn't looking good, is it? Still missing three days later. Best friend dead. It isn't looking good at all."

"Do you know anything about Michael's whereabouts?" Tom asked.

Barker looked shocked at such a direct question. "Me? Why would I know anything? I told you; I barely knew the boys."

"You said you photographed them climbing the hill," Ryan said.

"Well, yes. Look, don't get the wrong idea. I was taking some shots of the bridge and when I turned around, I saw two figures halfway up the hill, silhouetted against the sky. The light was perfect, so I took some pictures."

"How do you know it was Sam and Michael if you could only see silhouettes?" Ryan asked.

"Their bikes were on the trail below where they were climbing. I'd know those bikes anywhere. Seen them plenty of times. One of them is old, with a satchel on the back."

"Were the bikes lying on the ground?" Tom wondered if Barker had unknowingly photographed the boys while they were burying the necklace.

Barker shook his head. "They were leaning against a tree." He pointed. "One of those trees over there, in fact. The boys took care of their bikes, from what I saw. Why would they leave them on the ground?"

The trees Barker indicated grew near the base of the hill. They were the same trees Team Alpha had searched before ascending Stone Peak. A couple of yards away, at the edge of the river, was the spot where the marks had been found in the mud.

"What day was this?" Tom asked.

"Let's see…that would have been…" Barker closed his eyes as if trying to recall a memory. "…last week. It was definitely the end of the week. Was it Friday?" He shook his head. "No, not Friday." He opened his eyes again. "Thursday. It was Thursday evening."

"Are you sure?"

"Positive. I know it was Thursday because when I got home, my neighbour Mrs Higgins was having her shopping delivered. She has it delivered every Thursday."

Tom was dumbfounded. "So, you took photos of the boys three days before they disappeared and didn't report it to the police?"

Barker's eyes widened with shock. "Report it to the police? Why would I? They disappeared on Sunday, not Thursday."

"I want to see those photos," Tom said, pointing at the camera.

"You can't." Barker seemed flustered. "I mean, you can, but I can't show them to you at the moment. That isn't a digital camera, Inspector. I can't just press a button and show you the photos. I need to develop the film."

"We'll take the camera, then, and have the film developed at the police lab."

"What? No!" Barker stepped Between Tom and the tripod. "You can't just take my camera. Don't you need a...warrant or something?"

Tom hesitated. The photographer was right. Without a warrant, he couldn't confiscate the camera.

"Look, it's not a problem," Barker said. "I'll develop the film as soon as I get home and bring the relevant photos to the station. How does that sound?"

"I want every picture that pertains to this area and the people moving through here."

Barker grimaced. "The area, I can do, but people aren't my thing, I'm afraid. I take more than enough photos of people for work. Weddings, family portraits, that kind of thing. When I'm here on my own time, I'm all about the landscape and wildlife. That's why the camera is pointing at the riverbank over there. A kingfisher comes along here most days. I've been waiting here all morning for it to appear."

"Even if you're photographing the landscape, you must get people in the pictures sometimes," Ryan said.

Barker shrugged. "I try to avoid it, but there might be figures in the distance, I suppose."

"So, you'll get those photos to the station today." Tom made sure his words sounded like an order and not a question.

The photographer peered at the bank across the river and sighed. "I might as well pack up and go home, anyway. Doesn't look like the kingfisher is coming today. Don't worry, Inspector, you'll have your pictures by this afternoon." He began to dismantle the tripod.

"Thanks," Tom said. "We appreciate your cooperation."

He and Ryan continued along the path, leaving the photographer to pack away his gear. Fred followed them for a short distance, snuffling through the grass before turning around and returning to his owner.

"Barker seems a bit cagey, guv," Ryan said when they were out of earshot.

"Agreed," Tom wasn't sure what to make of the photographer's reluctance to hand over the camera. Even without a warrant, many people in the same situation would give the camera to the police voluntarily. Especially if it might contain evidence pertaining to the murder of one young boy and the disappearance of another.

"Think he's got something to hide?" Ryan was looking back along the path, as if trying to intuit Barker's character by merely staring at him.

"It's possible. He certainly didn't want us developing the film in that camera."

"Maybe he's been perving on the locals. Taking secret pictures from the bushes."

He nodded. "I wondered that myself."

"The dog would give him away, though. He couldn't stay hidden with Fred roaming around."

"We'll probably never know," Tom said. "The

photos he brings to the station will only be the ones he wants us to see."

"We could always get that warrant," she suggested. "Search his house for the rest."

"I doubt we'd manage to get a warrant. We'll see what Barker brings us and make a decision based on that. For now, we need to find this barn."

They reached the fork in the trail and took the path to the woods. Ryan led Tom through the trees to an old wire fence.

"This is the edge of George Gibbon's property," she said. "So, the barn should be somewhere along this fence line."

Tom glanced in both directions. The fence stretched about a mile to the West before meeting a stone wall, which Tom assumed marked the boundary of Wesley Brady's farm. There was no sign of any barn. To the East, the fence ran along the edge of the woods, hidden here and there by dense thickets, eventually curving out of sight.

"Let's go that way." Tom moved East, Ryan following close behind. Their progress was slow, because they had to fight their way around thick tangles of bushes and avoid fallen trees.

Tom kept the fence in sight at all times, skirting the farm's boundary as he made his way through the undergrowth.

DS Ryan moved much more nimbly, vaulting over fallen trees and expertly avoiding the hidden roots and holes in the ground that made Tom stumble.

"Go walking in the woods often, do you?" Tom said as he tripped on yet another tree root lurking beneath the undergrowth.

"I've loved the outdoors for as long as I can remember. My dad used to take me on nature walks when I was little, and ever since then, I've gone hiking or hill walking every chance I get." She hopped over a fallen branch and dodged a patch of nettles. "I take it you prefer the city."

"Is it that obvious?"

"Well, you were brought up in Relby, but you moved to London. That speaks volumes."

"I suppose it does." He wasn't about to trawl through his reasons for leaving, so he simply said, "The untamed wilderness isn't for me, I'm afraid. I like order. I'd rather live in a place that doesn't change wildly with each season. And I like the convenience of the city. Everything is accessible. Out here, you have to trudge along a muddy path or fight your way through brambles just to get anywhere."

As if to prove his point, a thorn-covered bush grabbed at his arm and tore a hole in his jumper. "See what I mean?" Tom said, exasperated. "That wouldn't happen on a city street."

DS Ryan tried hard to suppress a smile. She was obviously enjoying herself out here in nature. She seemed as at home here as Tom would be sitting in his local with a pint back in London.

She pointed at a field in the distance. "I think we've found the barn."

A ramshackle wooden structure sat in the long grass, partially hidden by wild, thorny bushes. A section of the roof had collapsed at some point in the past and the hole had been repaired with a blue tarpaulin which was now covered almost entirely by dark green moss. Wooden slats were missing from the walls and had never been replaced, leaving gaps large enough for a person to climb through.

There was no fence separating the overgrown field from the woods. Or at least there wasn't a fence here *now*. As Tom approached the field, he stepped over fallen fence posts that had rotted into the dirt. The wires that had once been attached to them were lost among the long grass.

Ryan deftly stepped over the hidden wires. "Looks like George Gibbon abandoned this part of his farm long ago."

They strode through the long grass towards the dilapidated structure. The day had become sunny and hot. Out in the open, exposed to the sun and no longer cooled by the shadows in the woods, Tom felt the heat burning through his clothing.

By the time he and Ryan reached the barn, he was sweating profusely.

Ryan crouched and peered through one of the gaps in the wall. "You'd better have a look at this, guv."

He crouched next to her and squinted against the gloom inside the barn. The air drifting out through the gap in the wall smelled of damp wood and mould, and something much worse. Tom wondered if the local animals came here to die.

When his eyes adjusted to the gloom, he realised why Ryan had wanted him to look inside.

Two bicycles were propped up against the far wall. One of the bicycles had a canvas saddlebag attached to its rear mudguard.

Tom reached into his pocket and took out the photograph of Sam and Michael's bikes. He held the picture out to DS Ryan. "Do you agree that the bicycles in this barn match the bicycles in the photo?"

She nodded. "The old bike with the saddlebag is unmistakable."

"Right." Tom fished his phone out of his pocket. "This area is now a crime scene."

CHAPTER
TWENTY

AN HOUR LATER, the Scenes of Crimes Officers had cordoned off the barn and entered the ramshackle building through an open doorway. The door had become detached from the structure at some point in the past and now lay rotting in the grass twenty feet away.

"It's someone with local knowledge," Tom said to DS Ryan, who stood next to him in the field, watching as the SOCOs carried out their work. "Whoever brought those bikes here knew this location."

The DS nodded in agreement. She'd gone quiet again. Tom wondered what she was thinking.

"Penny for 'em."

"I was just wondering how someone could bring two bikes here and not be noticed," she said. "We must be a couple of miles from the marks in the mud. Somebody wheeled both bikes along the path by the river and nobody saw anything?"

"There could be witnesses who haven't come forward," he reminded her. "People around here can be tight-lipped when they want to be."

The bicycles, wrapped in thick, transparent plastic, were brought out of the barn by Tyvek-suited SOCOs led by the gaunt figure of John Yorrick. Dried mud caked the handlebars. These were definitely the bikes that had been lying at the river's edge on Sunday evening.

"Yorrick!" Tom shouted. "There's probably a notebook in that saddlebag. I want photographs of every page. And I want them ASAP."

Yorrick gave a slight nod. His team continued their work, loading the bikes into the back of a four-wheel drive Land Rover, which was parked in the long grass. The SOCOs had entered the area via a narrow track at the top of the field, through a rusted metal gate that had been hanging off its hinges.

Tom wondered why George Gibbon had let this part of the farm go to rack and ruin. This could probably be good grazing land for cows. The farmer must have thought the barn too dangerous to let his animals near it.

"You think Sam's notebook will hold some answers?" Ryan asked.

Tom had no idea what the contents of the notebook would reveal. Perhaps nothing. There might be nothing more inside the so-called Mystery File than the nonsensical scribblings of two twelve-year-old boys. But there could be something else, perhaps something that would shed some light on what Sam and Michael were doing during the days leading up to the former's death and the latter's disappearance.

"I hope it holds some answers," he told Ryan. "We need them."

Yorrick came over to the edge of the cordon. "Looks like someone's been sleeping in there. There's an old mattress on the floor, candle stubs, some books. We'll test all of it, of course, but it's going to take some time."

"I realise that." Tom said. He'd spent many a frustrated hour waiting for lab results during his career so far and he was in no doubt there would be many more. Modern scientific methods of criminal detection were indispensable, but the delays that came with them were maddening, especially when someone's life could be on the line.

Yorrick returned to the barn.

At the top of the next field, a silhouetted figure stood watching them. Tom squinted his eyes against the light to make out the man's features but found it difficult to see any details. "Is that Wesley Brady?" he asked Ryan.

The DS shielded her eyes with her hand and nodded. "Yes, that's him." She waved and Brady waved back.

"How long has he been standing there?" Tom said. He was used to the general public rubbernecking at police affairs, but he wondered if Brady's interest was mere curiosity or something more.

"I don't know, guv, I didn't see him until now. I

suppose that's his field. This must be where his and George Gibbon's farms meet."

Remembering what his father had told him about Gibbon and Brady, Tom said, "Perhaps that's why Gibbon has let this field go to wrack and ruin. I understand there's no love lost between those two."

He watched the Land Rover make its slow journey through the long grass to the top of the field and past the broken gate. Then he looked over at the place Brady had been standing, but the farmer was gone.

It was early afternoon by the time they got back to the station. A young man in his twenties sat behind the front desk. Tom searched his memory for the name of the receptionist Hazel Owens had mentioned. Before it came to him, the young man stood up and offered his hand.

"Detective Inspector Brand, I'm Derek Flowers." He was thin, wearing a white shirt that hung loosely from his slight frame. A blue tie dangled from the oversized collar.

Tom shook the offered hand. Derek's grip was light as air.

"I'm DI Tom Brand, as you rightly guessed, and this is my colleague DS Kate Ryan."

"Oh, I didn't guess," Derek said. "I've seen you on the news. Both of you. I can't believe this tragedy happened the day we opened for business. It's heart breaking, it really is. Just goes to show they were right to put a station in Relby. I always said we needed more of a police presence around here."

Despite being part of that police presence, Tom didn't agree with the sentiment. Yes, a tragedy had occurred here —and there had been some trouble in the village's past— but that hardly meant Relby was a hotbed of crime. Once this case was closed, the station probably wouldn't be dealing with anything more serious than finding the occasional lost hiker or directing tourists to local landmarks. He'd spend the rest of his days killing time in the office, while yearning for his old career in London.

The front door opened, and Edward Barker bustled in, breathing heavily. When he saw Tom, he held out a manila envelope. "The photos you asked for are in there, Detective Inspector. Every landscape from my most recent roll of film."

Tom took the envelope. "Are you all right? You look flustered."

"I'm fine," Barker wiped his brow with a handkerchief before nodding at the envelope in Tom's hand. "You have what you asked for. You won't need to bother me again."

"We'll see about that." Tom wasn't about to let the photographer dictate terms. "If we need anything else, we'll be in touch. We know where to find you."

The photographer looked like he was about to say something but then changed his mind. He left the station without another word.

Tom led Ryan into his office. As the door closed behind them, he said, "He's hiding something. He couldn't get these pictures here fast enough. He made sure we didn't have to go to his house to pick them up."

"Agreed." Ryan gestured to the envelope in Tom's hand. "Shall we have a look at what he gave us?"

Tom emptied the envelope onto his desk. A number of black and white photos tumbled out. He arranged them into a rough rectangle. There were thirteen.

The picture that immediately stood out from the others showed the boys climbing Stone Peak, silhouetted against the sky as they ascended the steep, rocky hillside. There was no doubt that the dark figures in the photograph were Sam Jones and Michael Roberts. Tom had seen enough images of the boys to recognise them anywhere, even in silhouette.

He picked up the photo and placed it to one side, near Ryan.

She leaned over it to examine it more closely. "That's definitely the boys. The question is, did Barker take this photo on a whim, as he stated, or is it more sinister than that?"

"How many photos do you get on a roll of film?" Tom mused.

"Thirty-six, usually," Ryan said. "I was the proud owner of a Kodak camera when I was young. I used to take wildlife pictures with it. Some landscapes like these, but mostly birds and squirrels. I remember the rolls had thirty-six pictures on them because I had to wait for ages before I could get my pictures developed. I got so frustrated, I snapped pics of anything when I got near the end of the roll, just so I could see my photos."

"So, there are twenty-three photos missing," Tom said, gesturing to the thirteen pictures on the desk.

"Looks like it."

Other than the shot of the boys on Stone Peak, none of the photos had people in them. There were shots of the river, a few of the woods, and three pictures of a fallen tree that Barker seemed to have taken an interest in.

They were going to have to pay Barker another visit after all. Even if the other pictures from the roll were nothing more than portraits taken in Barker's studio, Tom wanted to see them. The thirteen pictures on the desk suggested an incompleteness that rankled him.

The desk phone rang, startling in the quiet of the office. Tom picked it up. "DI Brand."

The voice on the other end of the line was his father's. "Tom, I'm afraid I've had a bit of a fall. I'm in the hospital."

CHAPTER
TWENTY-ONE

THE THING that alarmed Tom the most when he entered the ward where his father was being treated was a deep purple bruise that covered almost half of the older man's face. His dad smiled sheepishly from his hospital bed, one eye almost lost in the dark, swollen socket.

"What happened, Dad?" Tom dropped into the bedside chair and placed a carrier bag of grapes and apples he'd bought on the way over here onto the tray table. He hadn't known what else to bring. You brought fruit to people in hospital, didn't you? That was the tradition, the done thing.

Before today, he'd only visited criminals in hospital, people who had hurt themselves carrying out some crime or other. He'd never had the urge to bring them anything other than the good news that they were going to be interviewed and charged.

"I was in the greenhouse," his dad said. "Tending to the tomatoes. The next thing I know, I'm lying on the ground with a tremendous pain shooting from my hip to my toes."

"You blacked out?"

His dad shrugged. He looked so frail in the hospital gown.

"What does the doctor say?"

"She wants to keep me in and run some tests. She thinks I might have fractured my hip."

Tom let out a slow breath. A fractured hip meant months of recovery, didn't it? His dad was already in enough pain without having to go through that as well.

"I'm sorry I'm such a burden, Tom."

"Nonsense. I'm just glad I'm here. You don't have to go through this alone. Is there anything you need from the house?"

"My toiletry bag and some clothes. Perhaps something to read. It's boring sitting here with nothing to do."

"Right. I'll be back in an hour." Tom stood up. At least he had a purpose and wasn't going to sit here uselessly.

When he got back to the house, he went straight up

to his father's bedroom but stopped in his tracks after he opened the door and stepped over the threshold.

The room looked exactly as it had when he'd been a child. Nothing had been changed; no furniture had been rearranged. His mother's dressing table sat near the window, and the streaming sunlight illuminated perfume bottles, and a silver-edged hand mirror Tom had given her as a birthday gift twenty years ago, bathing the table in an otherworldly glow.

On the bedside table, a framed photograph of his mother and father embracing and grinning at the camera during a holiday in Cancun sat beneath a Tiffany lamp whose stained-glass shade was decorated with dragonflies and red, orange and yellow Art Nouveau flowers.

Tom stood by the door, transfixed by something more than just the unchanged appearance of the space. Something deeper. The smell of his mother's perfume lingered in the air, as if she had just walked through the room.

He dropped onto the edge of the bed and put his hands over his face, surprised to feel tears on his cheeks. He'd been sixteen years old when his mother had left the house for the last time. She had driven away into a rainy night and never returned.

The memory of the sad-eyed policeman —one of his dad's work colleagues— arriving at the door was etched into Tom's memory. The accident had happened only two miles from the house. A drunk driver had drifted over the white line and hit his mother head on, instantly killing both her and himself.

After the funeral, Tom's thoughts had become fixated on one thing and one thing only: getting away from here. The following year, he applied to the Met, and when he was eighteen, he finally left Relby and its bad memories behind.

Returning to Derbyshire to look after his dad had made him wary of those memories resurfacing. Until now, he had managed to keep them buried. The job had focussed his thoughts on the missing boys and their families. But here in this room, the ghost of his mother was so present he felt she might appear before him suddenly and take him in her arms.

He got up from the bed and opened his father's wardrobe, finding a small, tartan suitcase inside. He placed it on the bed and filled it with a selection of casual clothing from the wardrobe and a toiletry bag containing his father's shaving kit from the bathroom.

A half-finished Patricia Cornwell novel lay on the bedside table, so Tom added that, as well as a handful of Agatha Christies and a couple of Dorothy L Sayers mysteries from the corner bookshelf. His dad might not be able to leave his hospital bed, but at least his mind could stay active.

He closed the suitcase and took it down to the car. Before he set off, he checked his face in the rearview mirror. His eyes were bloodshot but that should clear up before he got back to the hospital. He and his father rarely discussed his mother. An unspoken agreement seemed to have passed between them at some point. A mutual contract of silence. A contract written not in words, but in painful memories and raw emotion.

He started the car and drove back to the hospital, avoiding —as he always did— the road where his mother had died.

THURSDAY

CHAPTER
TWENTY-TWO

ON THURSDAY MORNING, Kate arrived at the station early. She booted up her computer and entered Wesley Brady's name into the police database. The results of the search took her by surprise. Brady had come into contact with the law on many occasions, mostly drunk and disorderly charges at the Mermaid, but the police had also been called out to his farmhouse on two occasions by Brady's wife Catherine. She had alleged that Brady had hit her, and Wesley had spent a night in jail on both occasions before Catherine had decided not to press charges.

All of that had happened a decade ago. Brady's record had been clean for the past eight years. Not even a speeding ticket. It looked like the man had turned his life around.

Kate checked the details of the first domestic disturbance and glanced at the name of the attending officer, then did a double take. She checked the name of the officer who had responded to the second disturbance. It was the same police constable. PC Francine Holt.

Was this why Holt was so interested in Wesley Brady? Because she'd met Brady all those years ago? What did that have to do with Sam Jones and Michael Roberts? What could it have to do with the boys? She racked her brains but came up with nothing. The domestic disturbance calls were ten years old. They had no connection to the current case.

So why was Holt, now a DCI, still interested in Brady? Why was she leaning on Kate for information about the man?

She closed the database and went upstairs to make a cup of tea. The upper floor of the station had been modernised with a kitchen, toilets, and staff breakout area complete with grey sofa and a glass coffee table. Half a dozen magazines lay on the table —*Cosmopolitan, Vogue, Elle,* and *Prima*. Kate hadn't seen them before. Perhaps Tilly had brought them, to read during her breaks.

Kate made the tea hot, strong, and sweet. She needed an extra boost of energy today. She took the drink downstairs and sat at her desk while she sipped it. She still hadn't heard from DI Brand other than a text last night saying his father was going to be staying in hospital. She hoped Max was going to be all right. She'd liked the man as soon as she'd met him, which was rare for her. She was usually much more guarded with new people.

Like she'd been with the DI himself. Since meeting

him, she'd evaluated his every decision, his every move, as if she were an invigilator and Brand were sitting an exam. He'd eventually passed with flying colours. Now, she had no reason to distrust him.

The door burst open, startling Kate from her reverie. Tilly blustered into the room with a folder under her arm. When she saw Kate, her face brightened. "Lovely morning!"

"Is it?" Kate glanced out of the window at the sun beating down on the fields. During the walk over here, she'd been so preoccupied with discovering why DCI Holt was interested in Wesley Brady that she hadn't noticed her surroundings. She still hadn't discovered the connection between Holt and Brady. The tiny nugget of information she'd uncovered was decades old. She needed to dig deeper, but had no idea where to—

"Are you all right?" Tilly dropped the folder onto her desk and collapsed into her chair. "You were away with the fairies."

"I'm fine. Just thinking about the case."

"I know what you mean. I've got a hundred door-to-door interviews to type up." She pulled a sheaf of handwritten pages out of the folder and leafed through them. "God knows how long it'll take me to get through this lot."

The door opened again, and Derek Flowers poked his head into the room. "There's a lady in Reception who says there's something wrong with her neighbour's dog. Apparently, it won't stop barking."

"No, I didn't say that," said a woman's voice from reception. "I said there must be something wrong with my neighbour because his dog is barking." She pushed past Derek and into the room. Kate immediately recognised her as the old woman who lived next door to Edward Barker. Her grey hair was still in rollers, and she wore a green wax jacket over a white flannel nightgown, her feet protected by nothing more than a pair of pink moccasin-style slippers.

"Edward Barker takes his dog Fred to the river every morning," she said, "but they haven't left the house, and Fred is barking like a lunatic. I'm telling you, something's wrong."

"Thanks, Derek," Kate said, dismissing the receptionist. "Come in, Mrs…"

"Mrs Eyre. Joan Eyre. And before you make a joke about my name sounding like Jane Eyre, I've heard them all. We need to get over to Edward's house and see what's wrong. I knocked on the door but all that did was send the dog into a frenzy. You're the police. You can break the door down."

It wasn't quite that simple, but Kate was willing to check on Barker if for no other reason than he might be connected to the case. "All right, let's go and have a look."

Edward Barker's house-cum-studio seemed exactly as it had yesterday. The bay window was intact and the front door with the *Edward Barker Photography. Weddings, Pets, Portraits* sign was firmly closed. The only difference was an incessant barking coming from within.

"That's Fred," Joan said.

Kate bent down and peered through the letterbox. She had a restricted view of a hallway that led to a closed door. The barking seemed to be coming from behind that door.

"Is there any way around the back?" she asked Joan.

The old woman frowned. "Not unless you go over my garden fence. But you don't need to do that, do you? You can use the big red key to smash the door down. You've got probable cause."

"A barking dog isn't reason enough to break the door down, Mrs Eyre."

"You'll have to climb over my fence into the back garden, then." Joan shook her head slowly. She obviously believed Kate was making the wrong decision by not forcing entry into the property immediately.

"All right," Kate said. At least if she got into Barker's back garden, she would have access to more windows and might be able to see what was wrong with the dog.

"Come on, then." Joan led the way next door and through her own house, which was decorated with floral wallpaper and smelled faintly of roses. The back door was situated in the kitchen at the back of the house. A flat cap and black work jacket hung on a hook next to the door.

"Those belonged to Frank, my husband," Joan said. "Couldn't bear to part with them after he passed." She opened the door onto a paved garden filled with wooden planters and potted flowers.

Kate went outside and examined the fence. Standing eight feet tall and made of thick wood, it looked sturdy enough to take her weight. Stepping onto the edge of a rose planter, she boosted herself up and peered into Barker's back garden.

The photographer's garden consisted of an overgrown lawn bordered by untidy bushes, tangled weeds, and a large ceramic plant pot that might once have housed flowers but was now full of nothing more than dead grass.

Fred's cries sounded louder from back here; the dog was clearly in the kitchen. Kate pulled herself up with her arms and swung a leg over the fence, letting gravity take her over into the overgrown garden. Instead of landing gracefully, as she'd intended, she ended up sitting among the weeds with a bruised ego, if nothing else.

Dusting broken stalks and seed pods from her trousers, she approached the kitchen window and looked inside. Fred was sitting by the radiator, his lead looped around the hot water pipe so he couldn't move more than a few feet in any direction. When he saw Kate, he howled.

"It's okay, Fred. We'll get you out of there." She tried

the back door, surprised when it opened. On closer inspection, she saw why. The frame was splintered near the handle. Someone had forced the door open.

Kate entered the kitchen and unhooked the lead from Fred's collar. The dog sprinted outside and relieved himself among the bushes. Kate closed the door. Fred didn't seem aggressive, but he might try to guard his home when she entered the rest of the house.

Opening the door to the hallway, she called, "This is the police. Is anyone in this house?"

The only sound was the rhythmic ticking of a clock coming from another room. Kate checked that room. The clock was a cuckoo clock on a wall filled with framed black and white landscape photographs. The room itself had been converted into a studio. A dark blue backdrop hanging from a frame dominated the space, along with various lights on stands. A tripod sat in front of the backdrop but there was no camera attached to it. Stolen, maybe? Of perhaps Barker kept the camera somewhere else in the house.

The drawers of a filing cabinet had been pulled open and various documents tossed onto the floor. Had this been a burglary? If so, where was Edward Barker?

She went back to the hallway and called up the stairs, "Mr Barker, are you here?"

The clock continued to tick in the studio.

She should probably call this in; she was walking through a crime scene, contaminating evidence. But Edward Barker might be in need of immediate medical attention. The dog had been tied up unharmed in the kitchen but what if Barker was in a worse state upstairs? He could be bleeding out. Any hesitation on Kate's part might cost him his life.

She took the stairs two at a time and reached a landing strewn with photographs. An open door revealed a darkroom complete with developing tanks and a wire line where photos might have hung while developing, but which was now empty. Dozens of photos lay on the floor, spilling out onto the landing. This was no ordinary burglary; someone had been looking for something specific.

Kate had no idea whether the intruder had found what they were looking for or not, or if they were still in the house. She stepped over the mess of photos to a closed door and pushed it open.

This was Barker's living room. Since he had converted the house's actual living room into a studio, he'd obviously changed one of the bedrooms into a living area. A sofa sat beneath the window, facing a TV on the opposite wall. A plush dog bed lay on the floor next to the sofa and two dog bowls, each labelled *Fred* sat on the floor of a kitchenette area which contained little more than a kettle, microwave, small fridge, and air fryer. The kitchen cupboards were all open. The drawers of a bureau, which was the only other furnishing in the living area except for the sofa, had been opened and searched. Most of their contents — papers, pens, and other odds and ends— had been tossed onto the floor.

No sign of Barker.

Kate moved back onto the landing. Other than an empty bathroom, whose door was open, there was only one room she had not yet entered. The door to the bedroom situated at the front of the house was closed.

Kate approached it and called, "Mr Barker, are you in there? It's the police."

Silence.

She opened the door. The curtains were closed, the room shrouded almost in complete in darkness. Light spilling in from the hallway revealed a bed and a bedside table whose drawers had been ransacked. As Kate stepped forwards, her attention was caught by a bulky shape lying on the floor at the foot of the bed.

As she got closer, she understood what the shape was. Edward Barker lay face down in a pool of blood that had soaked into the carpet and his pyjamas. The back of the pyjama top was ripped open, revealing bloody wounds striping Barker's back. Kate knelt down and checked for a pulse, even though she knew there was no way Barker could still be alive after losing so much blood. His flesh was cold. There was no pulse. He was long past medical assistance.

She stepped back carefully, trying not to touch anything else in the room. When she got downstairs, she fought back bile rising in her throat. If she vomited, she would really contaminate the scene. Yorrick's team would kill her.

The darkly humorous thought dragged her mind from the compulsion to vomit, but only for a few seconds. She rushed out into the back garden and leaned against the house with both hands, gulping in fresh air while her stomach settled.

Fred padded up to her, wagging his tail and whining.

"It's all right, boy," she said, stroking him behind his ears. "It's all right."

But it wasn't. It wasn't all right at all. Kate pulled her phone out of her pocket and called it in.

CHAPTER
TWENTY-THREE

TOM GOT to the station later than usual because he'd visited his father before breakfast. Still no news other than the fact that an x-ray had been scheduled for later in the day. He entered the office to find Tilly typing up reports, but no Ryan.

"Is DS Ryan here?" he said.

Tilly looked up from her screen. "She's gone to see a man about a dog."

Tom frowned, confused. Was she having him on? "What do you mean?" he ventured.

"Jane Eyre came in and said her neighbour's dog was barking, so DS Ryan went to have a look." She paused, her brows furrowing as she tried to remember something. "Sorry, not Jane Eyre. *Joan* Eyre. Funny things, names. Not only that, the man whose dog was barking is named Barker. Isn't that funny?"

"Edward Barker?"

Tilly pursed her lips for a moment. "Yes, that's him.

The guy whose address I found yesterday. Church Street, wasn't it?"

Tom fished his phone out of his jacket pocket. He had three missed calls from DS Ryan. He'd turned the bloody ringer off in the hospital and forgotten to turn it on again when he'd left. He called her.

Ryan picked up immediately. "There's been a development, guv. Edward Barker is dead."

"How?"

"Someone broke into his house and murdered him in his bedroom. The SOCOs are here gathering evidence."

Realisation hit Tom suddenly. Edward Barker was dead. Murdered. They'd spoken to him only yesterday and now he'd been killed. Was his murder connected to the case?

"You still there, guv?"

"Yes. I'm coming over. I'll be there in as minute." He ended the call and left the station, his thoughts still reeling with the implications of Barker's death. There had to be a connection to Sam Jones and Michael Roberts. Coincidences happened, but this was way beyond a chance occurrence. Some sort of thread connected Barker to the boys, and to an unknown person who had probably killed all three of them. But why? Why kill the boys and then go after Barker?

When he got to Church Street, he sighed inwardly. Reporters and bystanders crowded the police tape cordon that surrounded the photographer's house. The news of Barker's death had obviously spread through the village like wildfire.

All eyes were on him as he approached the crime scene. He heard someone whisper, "That's the detective from the new police station."

A microphone was shoved in front of his face by a female reporter. "Detective Inspector Brand, is this murder related to the Sam Jones and Michael Roberts case?"

"No comment." He ducked under the tape, which was held aloft by a uniformed officer, and made his way to the open front door of the house.

A Scenes of Crime Officer in the hallway handed him a white Tyvek suit. "You'll need to put this on, sir."

Tom nodded and quickly donned the suit before entering the house. "Is Detective Sergeant Ryan here?" he asked the SOCO.

"She's in the garden, sir."

Tom trod carefully along the hallway and through the kitchen to the back door. Ryan was sitting on the edge of a large plant pot in the middle of the overgrown lawn. Her eyes were fixed on the ground in front of her and she looked pale.

"Are you all right?" he asked, making sure to stay inside the doorway. The SOCOs would be none too pleased if he went out into the garden and brought soil back inside on the soles of the Tyvek foot coverings.

She looked up and shrugged. "I'll be fine, guv. It was just a bit of a shock, that's all."

"You think this was a burglary gone wrong? Or

something more than that?" He already knew the answer, but keeping Ryan talking would help her shake off the shock she was experiencing.

"It wasn't a burglary," she said. "Someone was looking for something specific. There are photos scattered all over the landing, and all the drawers have been gone through."

"Do you think it's connected to our case?"

"I would say so. We spoke to Barker yesterday and now he's dead. That's too much of a coincidence for my liking."

"Agreed. The question is: how is this all connected?"

Ryan shrugged again.

"What happened to Barker's dog?"

"Fred is at the local vets, being checked over."

"Is he all right?"

"I think so. I found him tied to the kitchen radiator. Other than that, he didn't seem to have been harmed at all. The SOCOs went over his fur and paws with a vacuum and then the vet came to pick him up."

If only animals could talk. Knowing who had broken in and killed Barker might break the Sam Jones and Michael Roberts case wide open.

"Good job, Ryan. Get yourself back to the station. I'll meet you there in a bit." He wanted to see the scene upstairs for himself, get a feel for what had happened here.

The DS nodded and gestured to the garden fence. "I'll go back via next door; the same way I got in."

"All right, I'll see you later." Tom retraced his steps

along the hallway and ascended the stairs. The floor above was buzzing with activity as SOCOs scoured every inch of the landing and adjacent rooms, collecting evidence and sealing it in clear plastic bags.

"Where's the body?" Tom said to no one in particular.

An officer collecting photographs from the landing floor pointed at the front bedroom. "In there, sir." The bedroom door was open, the room crowded with white-suited officers.

Yorrick was in there, directing his team. When he saw Tom, he said, "Give the detective some room." The SOCOs moved aside to allow Tom entry.

"We've taken photographs already," Yorrick said as Tom entered the room. "We'll send the body for a post-mortem examination soon and continue collecting trace evidence in here."

The first thing Tom noticed was a copper-tinged, rancid smell hanging in the air. Edward Barker's body lay face down on the bedroom floor, covered in bloody wounds and slashes that seemed to have been made with a knife blade.

"Any wounds on his front?" he asked Yorrick.

Yorrick shook his head. "He was stabbed from behind while lying in bed. You see the bloodstain there and how it leads down the mattress to the foot of the bed? I'd say our victim tried to crawl out of bed and was stabbed repeatedly as he did so. Eleven times, to be exact. He was dead before he hit the floor. Quite a vicious attack."

Tom tried to visualise the scene, an easy task with Barker's body lying right in front of him. The photographer never had a chance. "Was the house searched before or after the murder?"

"It looks like after. Items from the bedside table were sitting on top of the bloodstains."

"So, Barker didn't interrupt a burglar," Tom mused. "The motive was murder all along."

"Motives are your area of expertise, Inspector. I'm just here to pick up the pieces and try to make sense of the mess."

Tom nodded. He'd seen enough. The perpetrator was looking for something in the house but also wanted Edward Barker dead. How any of this was connected to the boys, he had no idea.

"However," Yorrick continued, "the intruder may have been looking for this. We found it taped to the underside of the bed." He picked up an evidence bag from the bedside table and handed it to Tom.

Inside the bag was something wrapped tightly in black plastic and clear tape. It felt light in Tom's hand and was no larger than a thin paperback book.

"We'll open it at the lab after checking it for prints," Yorrick said, "But I don't think the intruder touched this. If he had, he'd probably have taken it with him when he left."

Tom had to agree. Whatever was bound in the black plastic and tape, Barker had thought it valuable enough to hide underneath the bed.

He handed the evidence bag back to Yorrick. "Let me know as soon as you open it."

The SOCO said, "Of course. Also, I've had a copy of that notebook we found in the bicycle saddlebag sent over to the station. It should be waiting on your desk by now."

"Thanks."

"There was nothing interesting on the notebook itself. Prints from both boys, of course, but that's about it. We're still going over the bikes."

"What about the contents of the notebook?"

"I have no idea, Inspector. I simply had my team photocopy the pages and bind the copies into a facsimile of the original. We're checking the pages for prints, but I haven't read them. As I said, my job is to pick up the pieces. The rest is up to you."

CHAPTER
TWENTY-FOUR

WHEN HE GOT BACK to the station, Tom found DS Ryan sitting at her desk, concentrating on her computer screen, looking much more composed than she had in Barker's garden. Tilly was likewise occupied at her own desk, typing up reports.

He went to his office and dropped into his chair, rubbing his eyes. It had been a long day already, and it only lunchtime.

A large manila envelope sat on the desk with his name clearly written on a white label beneath a red stamp that read, *Confidential*.

He tore it open and pulled out a sheaf of photocopied pages that had been bound together and sandwiched between black plastic cover sheets to form a small book. Tom opened the cover. A handwritten title page read:

Mystery File
Property of Sam Jones

The neat handwriting looked like it had been made with a pen. Tom turned the page.

Michael came over after school and we had a meeting about the Stone Peak Mystery. We agreed that we need to watch the suspect closely for any more suspicious activity. We are going to build a hideout so we can observe him without being seen. When the summer holidays get here, we can spend more time in the hideout and solve this mystery once and for all.

The Stone Peak Mystery. It would be easy to dismiss those words as nothing more than the product of a young boy's imagination. But now, with Sam dead and Michael unaccounted for, it seemed entirely possible that the boys had stumbled onto something real.

The first passage had mentioned that the Summer Holiday hadn't started yet, so it could have been written any time before last week. But how long before?

A week? A month? Tom liked facts. He needed solid data to do his job properly. Frustratingly, this notebook seemingly offered none of those things.

He flipped the page.

> *The hideout is finished. We used branches and mud and string to build it just like it said in Michael's survival book. And we brought biscuits and pop to celebrate. Fred had some biscuits as well.*

Tom sat up in his chair. Fred. Was that a reference to Edward Barker's dog, or did the boys know someone else called Fred? Another child, perhaps? The entry was too vague to be useful.

He closed his eyes and pinched the bridge of his nose. A headache loomed, making the back of his skull feel heavy. *I have to manage my expectations regarding this notebook. It was written by a twelve-year-old who had no ideas his words would later be examined by a detective.*

He got up and went to the whiteboard on his office wall. Taking a blue pen from the tray at the base of the board, he wrote: *Timeline* and beneath the word, he drew a long horizontal line from one edge of the board to the other. Maybe he could piece together a timeline from Sam's notes. Even if it wasn't complete, it would be something concrete.

On the right side of the timeline, he drew a small vertical line and labelled it:

Sam's body found in river.

On the left, he made a similar line and wrote:

Boys build hideout to observe "suspect."
Suspect is male.

As for the rest, he would try to piece the events together from the scant information in the notebook.

In red pen, further down the board, he wrote,

Fred ???

Could the name refer to Barker's dog? Had the photographer been with the boys in their hideout?

Tom went to the open office door and said, "Tilly, I need you to contact the Family Liaison Officers working with the Jones and Roberts families. Find out if the boys knew anyone named Fred. A friend from school, maybe. In fact, contact the school and see if there are any students named Fred or Frederick."

Tilly looked up from her screen. "The school is closed for the summer, sir."

He'd forgotten about that. "Right. Track down a member of staff, then. Someone who knows the names of all the students."

"Yes, sir. Student named Fred. Got it." She picked up a pen and scribbled on a Post-it note. "Can I ask you a question, sir?"

"Of course."

"What's going to happen to Fred the dog?"

"I don't know. I assume he'll be re-homed or go to one of Edward Barker's family members. Don't worry, Tilly, he'll be looked after."

She nodded and turned her attention back to the computer.

Tom returned to the notebook. As he settled into his chair, ready to learn more about Sam's amateur detective work, the desk phone rang.

He picked up the receiver and cradled it against his shoulder while he drew a timeline identical to the one on the whiteboard in his own notebook. "DI Brand."

"John Yorrick," the voice on the other end said. "We've opened the package we found under Edward Barker's bed. There are quite a few photographs inside."

"Photographs of what?"

"The boys are in some of them, shots taken outdoors from a distance. But most of the other pictures are just… meaningless, as far as I can see. I'll get them uploaded to the digital case file later today."

"Thanks."

"There's something else. We've checked the bicycles for fingerprints. Sam's and Michael's prints are all over them, of course, but we also found two unknown sets of adult-sized prints on each bicycle."

"The boys' parents?"

"No, we've got elimination prints from them. These prints are from other people, and they aren't in the system. Two separate sets, and both were made with muddy fingers. Same mud from the riverside location where the marks on the ground indicate the bikes had been lying."

Tom let that sink in. Two assailants?

"Anyway," Yorrick said, "It will all be in my report, but I thought I'd let you know."

"Thanks, I appreciate it."

Yorrick hung up. Tom did the same, and wrote,

Two sets of unknown adult prints on bikes

in his notebook. It was the word *unknown* that bothered him. Fingerprints were useless unless there was a suspect to match them to. Did a set of these prints belong to the "suspect" Sam had referred to in the notebook?

If so, who did the other set belong to?

His skull felt like it was tightening more and more with each passing second. The office felt stuffy. The entire station still smelled annoyingly of fresh paint. He needed to get out of here.

Picking up the facsimile Mystery File and his own notebook, he left the office. "Ryan, what are you up to?"

She looked up from her computer. "Just checking over some details of the case, guv."

"Fancy a trip out?"

"Definitely." She logged out of her computer and followed him out of the station. "Where are we going?" she asked as they walked across the car park.

"Anywhere. I need some fresh air; the paint smell is giving me a headache."

"Right. I'll drive. I've got painkillers in the car."

She slid in behind the wheel of her Jeep and said, "Painkillers are in the glove box, guv."

Tom got in and opened the glove box, discovering a tub of paracetamol and a packet of ibuprofen among an assortment of tissue packets, throat lozenges, and a variety of chocolate bars and sweets.

"Looks like you're well-stocked with all the necessities," he said as he opened the paracetamol.

"It's a habit I've had since childhood. I like to be ready for anything." She reached into the backseat and handed him a bottle of spring water. "It comes in handy sometimes."

He swallowed the bitter-tasting painkillers while Ryan guided the Jeep out of the car park and onto the main road.

"Do you think we've missed anything, guv?" she asked.

"There's a lot we don't know, but I don't think we've missed anything," he said. "Why, what are you thinking?"

She shrugged noncommittally. "The people we've interviewed. What if they know more than they're saying?"

He rubbed the bridge of his nose with his thumb and forefinger and closed his eyes. The painkillers hadn't kicked in yet, and Ryan's question did nothing to help alleviate the stress he felt. "Do you have someone specific in mind?"

"Wesley Brady," the DS said. "I've looked into his background. He's got a history of suspected domestic abuse against his ex-wife, and a number of drunk and disorderly arrests."

Tom remembered what his father had said regarding Brady's unhappy marriage to Catherine but didn't see how that could have any bearing on the current case. "I'm not seeing a connection," he told Ryan.

"I'm not saying there *is* a connection," she said. "But we can't take these people at face value. They have skeletons in their closets. Secrets from the past."

"Everyone has skeletons in their closet, Ryan; you've been a detective long enough to know that. Brady's trouble with the law doesn't mean he murdered Sam Jones."

"I know." She sighed, and there was frustration in the sound. "I just want to make sure we're not overlooking something."

"I want to solve this case as much as you do, but we have to do it methodically, with facts. Following hunches and dead-end leads will get us nowhere. We focus our efforts on solid evidence. Speaking of which, Yorrick's team photocopied the Mystery File and put it all in here." He held up the black plastic-covered notebook.

The DS's eyes widened as she glanced over at it before turning her attention back to the road. "Have you read it? What does it say?"

"I've only looked at some of it. The boys built a hideout to observe someone they referred to as "the suspect." It also mentions someone named Fred being at the hideout."

"Fred the dog? Edward Barker's dog?"

"I'm not sure. That's why I asked Tilly to look into the possibility of a schoolmate with the same name."

"Seems a bit coincidental. It's probably the dog, which means Barker was at the hideout as well."

Tom nodded. "That's the most likely explanation."

"I don't like the way this is going, guv."

"Neither do I."

Ryan drove them out of the village and along winding roads Tom wasn't familiar with. They gained elevation, which afforded them a view of the surrounding hills and moors. Tom supposed the view would be considered spectacular by the many tourists who flooded here every year, but to him this place only served as a reminder that life was short and loved ones could be snatched away at any moment. A country road, a rain-filled night, a drunk driver, a life lost. That was the only thing he thought of when he saw the rolling landscape. This place had taken his mother, and he hated it for that.

"Where are we going?" he asked Ryan, turning his gaze away from the window.

"I'm taking you to my favourite pub," she told him.

"Do they serve food?"

"The best in Derbyshire."

"All right, we'll see about that." He hadn't realised how hungry he was until now, and the thought of some good pub grub made his stomach rumble.

Ryan laughed. "Would I lie to you, guv?"

"I'll let you know once I've tasted their cottage pie."

Twenty minutes later, they arrived at a sprawling stone building that clung to the top of a high hill. A wooden sign proclaimed the building to be the Willows Inn, established in 1724. With small leaded windows and a low roof, the pub looked sturdy enough to withstand whatever the elements threw at it up here, and the fact that it had stood on this hill since the 18th century attested to that.

Ryan parked the Jeep near the front entrance —a heavy oak door with a brass plaque that read *Welcome to the Willows Inn*— and climbed out of the car. "I'm buying," she said.

Inside, the Willows had all the character and cosiness that Tom expected in a three-hundred-year-old pub. A fire crackled in a huge stone fireplace, its smoky scent mingling with the strong smell of beer and cooked food. Dark wooden beams supported a low ceiling, and similarly exposed beams ran along the walls. The pub was full, and the clatter of cutlery along with animated chatter made the place feel alive.

Tom found a table in the corner, next to a window that looked out over the car park, while Ryan went to the bar to order their food. She returned with two soft drinks and slid one across the table towards him. "Cottage pie coming up, guv" she said before taking a sip of her Coke.

"I look forward to it." The mouth-watering smell of food emanating from the kitchen told him the pie was going to be one of the best he had ever tasted.

"How's the headache?"

"Almost gone, thanks to the painkillers."

She gestured at the facsimile Mystery File, which he had brought into the pub. "Some light lunchtime reading?"

"I thought we could have a quick look at it while we're waiting for the food."

She held out her hand expectantly. "May I?"

He passed her the notebook and sat back while she flicked through the pages.

Ryan stared at the pages for a few seconds before frowning. She turned a couple of pages over and frowned again before flicking through the notebook more quickly, a confused look on her face. She looked at Tom. "You didn't read past the first couple of pages, did you?"

"No, I didn't. Why? What does it say?"

She handed the open notebook back to him. "You tell me."

He looked down at the page and felt a sinking feeling in his stomach. Instead of words, the page was filled with row after row of stick figures that had been drawn in various positions. Tom leafed through the notebook and found more of the same on every page. Hundreds of stick figures populated the book. The only pages with actual writing on them were the ones Tom had read in the station.

So, there was no "Stone Peak Mystery" after all. Sam Jones had simply filled the Mystery File with these drawings. What might have been a useful lead was nothing more than a notebook full of meaningless doodles.

Or was it? Were the doodles meaningless? He looked closer at the figures. They had been drawn carefully, the positions of their arms and legs placed precisely on the page. Those positions, which he had at first thought random, repeated at various intervals. The arrangement of the stick figures seemed to mean something.

He looked at Ryan and said, "It's written in code."

She raised an eyebrow. "Are you sure?"

"Look at the arrangement of the figures; it isn't random. There's a pattern here."

She examined the drawings and nodded. "Yes, I see it. The question is, how do we find out what it means?"

"I don't think we're going to solve it ourselves over lunch. We need to find a professional codebreaker, if such a person exists."

"I'm sure they do, but they probably work in secret for the government."

"We need to find someone local, even if it's just an enthusiastic amateur. We need to know what this says."

The food arrived, interrupting the conversation. Tom closed the notebook and moved it to the side of the table to make room for his cottage pie, which came with chips and a fresh side salad. He added salt and vinegar to the chips before taking a bite of the pie. Ryan's assessment of "the best food in Derbyshire" might just be accurate. The deep, rich flavour of the beef mince, onion, and carrots was offset perfectly by a fluffy mashed potato topping which melted in his mouth.

"I told you it was good," Ryan said, watching his reaction closely.

"You weren't lying. How do you know about this place? It's in the middle of nowhere."

"My dad used to bring me here when I was younger. He and my mum found it before they were married and came here all the time. That table over there is where they usually sat, and where he and I sat after she died."

Tom hadn't known Ryan's mother was dead. "I'm sorry for your loss."

"She died when I was very young," Ryan said. "I used to think I might feel a connection to her in this pub, since she came here a lot, but I've never felt anything. Even sitting in her seat at the table she shared with Dad. Nothing." Her eyes went to the window. Tom took that to mean this particular conversation was over, which was fine with him. He hadn't meant to upset Ryan, and as he took another bite of the cottage pie, he tried to think of a new topic of to steer the conversation in a different direction.

But as Ryan pulled her gaze from the window and resumed eating, she said, "She died on Kinder Scout twenty-five years ago. There was a really bad storm. I still wonder why the hell she went up there. It was New Year's Day; she should have spent it with her family. Then she might still be here instead of leaving us to live our lives without her."

She sniffed and wiped her eyes with the back of her hand, clearly holding back tears.

"I lost my mother when I was sixteen," Tom said. It was something he never spoke of, and the words surprised him even as they left his mouth, but he wanted Ryan to know that he understood her pain. "She was in a head-on collision with a drunk driver. My dad and I have never been the same since, even all these years later. We hardly ever speak about her. And when we do, there's an underlying tension between us. I think he resents the fact that I moved to London as soon as I could after her death and left him to deal with the aftermath." He shoved a chip into his mouth to shut himself up. He was definitely oversharing now and that was something he never did, especially where his mother's death was concerned.

It was Ryan's turn to offer a condolence. "I'm sorry to hear that. Losing your mum is terrible, but her death driving a wedge between you and your dad makes it even worse."

"It is what it is," Tom said. The situation between himself and his father had been going on for so long now that it had become the status quo.

"I sometimes fall out with my family as well," Kate said. "They all think my mum made an error in judgement when she went out into that storm, but I can't come to terms with that. There has to be more to it than just a simple mistake." Her eyes went to the window again. Tom got the impression she was looking at something more than the car park. Something in her mind's eye.

"When I was sixteen," she continued, "I climbed Kinder Scout, looking for some kind of connection to her. But there was nothing. Nothing at all. I stood on the summit in the pouring rain, and I just felt lost and alone. Everything up there was so bleak. I wondered how my mum had felt in her final moments. Had she felt alone? Were her final thoughts of me and Dad waiting for her at home?"

She turned her face from the window. "I'll never know. And I'll never know *her*. She wasn't there for any of the events in my life. Graduation. Becoming a detective. My entire life changed the day she went up that hill. My dad's, too. Something so terrible has to be the result of more than just a simple mistake."

Tom nodded his understanding but said nothing. In his line of work, he'd seen too many lives shattered by mistakes. Fatal road traffic accidents caused by a driver believing it was safe to overtake another car when it wasn't. Pedestrians stepping off the kerb at the wrong moment and ending up under the wheels of a bus. Swimmers drowned in rivers because they'd mistakenly thought the water shallow or the current weaker than it actually was.

He had no doubt that Ryan had seen similar tragedies during her time on the force and knew that mistakes could have fatal consequences. Yet where her own mother's death was concerned, it seemed she needed to believe in something more than a simple lapse in judgement.

It wasn't his place to disabuse her of that notion.

They ate a couple more mouthfuls, then Kate said, "Can I ask you something personal?"

He wasn't sure how to answer that. "Okay," he said warily.

She cleared her throat, as if giving herself time to formulate the question. "Don't take this the wrong way. I'm not questioning your actions, I'm just curious."

Now *he* was curious. He leaned toward her over the table slightly. "Go on."

"You said you moved to London as soon as you could after your mother's death."

"That's right."

Kate narrowed her eyes slightly and looked down at her plate, as if to soften the blow of what she was about to say by not confronting him directly. "Do you think you were running away?"

He said nothing for a moment. It was a question he sometimes asked himself but never expected to hear from someone else's lips. The answer he gave Kate was the same one he always told himself in those moments of self-reflection. "No, of course I wasn't running away. I wanted to work in the city, to be a police officer in the Met and climb the ladder to become a detective. The best way to do that is to join at a young age."

She looked up at him and nodded. He wasn't sure she believed his answer.

"I'm sorry if that was too personal—" she began.

He cut her off. "No, it's fine. I can understand why you might think that. It was bad timing, that's all. My mother died just as I was about to embark on my career. I can see how it might look like I was running away from everything, but I was simply following the career path I'd been working toward since realising I wanted to be a copper."

He suspected that last part was a lie. He couldn't remember harbouring a desire to move to London and join the Met until *after* his mother's death. He had wanted to join the police force long before then, but hadn't his goal been to become a detective somewhere in the countryside? Had the accident changed everything and put the thought of London in his head?

They ate the rest of the meal in silence and when

they were finished, Tom sat back and said, "That was amazing. Thank you."

"Glad you liked it, guv."

"Time to get back to the station." He stood up and stretched, wincing as his back cracked. "We need to find someone who can break that code."

CHAPTER
TWENTY-FIVE

POLICE CONSTABLE MARK BARNES had been looking forward to his new job as a village copper. His dream was to walk his beat in an area where everyone would eventually get to know him and see him as a friendly face, unlike his previous policing job in Manchester where he had been largely ignored by the locals unless they were hurling insults at him.

Being assigned to the new police station in Relby had made that dream come true. A chance for a fresh start after the turmoil of the city. The case of the missing boys meant he'd had an unusual first few days on the job —being part of a search team instead of walking the village beat— but today he had finally been tasked to perform what would become his regular duty. It was time to show his face to the people of Relby and earn their trust.

As he walked past the Mermaid pub, he nodded a greeting to everyone on the street and offered them a wide smile. His mother often lamented the demise of the friendly bobby on the beat, something that had been common back in her day, and something PC Barnes was determined to bring back to life.

He was lost in his thoughts of bringing the friendly face of policing to the village of Relby when a middle-aged man ran out of the Newsagent's, saw Mark, and shouted, "Police! Help!"

Mark became focused immediately. Duty called. He was needed. "What's wrong, sir?"

The man, whose dark blue shirt was embroidered with the words *Tobin's Newsagent's* in yellow script-like writing, looked panicked. His eyes were wide and full of confusion. "My shop is being wrecked." He pointed at the establishment. Through the window, Mark could see a shadowy figure pulling items off the shelves and tossing them to the floor.

"Wait here, sir. I'll deal with this." He pulled the telescopic baton from his belt and extended it to its full length. Although the directive for the baton was to resort to the weapon's use only when in a dangerous situation, Mark mentally justified his own actions by telling himself this *was* a dangerous situation. The person inside the shop was heavyset and clearly out of control. Mark would be lucky to come out of this encounter unscathed.

He thumbed his radio and called for backup before striding forward toward the shop door. As soon as he opened it, he heard screaming coming from within. The person wrecking the joint seemed to be in a fit of rage.

Mark could see the young man now. He looked to be in his twenties, wearing a tan baseball cap and a blue *Fortnite* t-shirt and shorts. The floor was littered with newspapers, magazines, chocolate bars, and bags of crisps, and the young man was in the process of sweeping more chocolate bars from the shelves with one arm. Tears ran down his face and his mouth was twisted into a snarl. The sound escaping his throat was a guttural scream of pain.

Mark held up a placating hand in an attempt to defuse the situation, keeping the baton behind him in the other hand. "Hey, stop that right now."

The young man halted momentarily, his tear-filled eyes finding Mark.

"Calm down," Mark said. "Whatever the problem is, we can talk about it."

"They're dead," the young man said. His teeth clenched and his eyes widened with fury. He pulled a box of chocolate bars from the shelf and flung it to the ground. "They're dead!" he repeated.

Mark had to control the situation. He moved forward purposefully, bringing the baton forward with as much force as he could muster in the confined space. He remembered his training —target the large muscle groups— and slammed the weapon into the man's thigh, hoping to bring him down.

The attack elicited a scream of rage but nothing further from the young man. He did not go down as Mark had hoped. Instead, he threw a handful of Double Deckers into Mark's face.

Right, that was it. Enough was enough. Mark moved determinedly and swung the baton again, rapping it across his opponent's chest. The young man stumbled, and this time he *did* go down, landing heavily among the discarded crisp packets and chocolate bars on the floor.

Mark pulled his cuffs from his belt and moved quickly, dropping to his knees to secure the man's arms behind his back. "You're under arrest for criminal damage. You do not have to say anything. But it may harm your defence if you do not mention, when questioned, something which you later rely on in court. Anything you do say may be given in evidence."

The only response was tears. The offender's chest and back heaved as he sobbed.

"Come on," Mark said, getting to his feet. "Let's go outside and get some fresh air."

He helped the young man get to his feet and took him outside. There was no resistance now, only tears.

The newsagent came over, a look of concern on his face. "Charlie, are you all right?"

The offender nodded but said nothing.

"You two know each other?" Mark asked.

"Of course." The newsagent frowned at the question as if it were ridiculous. "Charlie is a regular in my shop."

"What's your last name, Charlie?" Mark asked the young man.

"Gibbon." The reply came through tears and sniffs.

Mark took out his notebook and wrote the name down. "And your name, sir?" he asked the newsagent.

"Frank Tobin."

"You said he's a regular at your shop, Mr Tobin. Has he ever done this before?"

"No, never."

"So, what was different today?"

"I just told him I was sorry to hear about Sam Jones and Michael Roberts. I know the boys are his friends. *Were* his friends, I mean."

"And that provoked the outburst?"

Tobin nodded. "Charlie's got learning disabilities. He doesn't react to things the way other people do. I suppose I shouldn't have mentioned his friends, but I thought he already knew. Now I've got to tidy up." He sighed wearily and went back into the shop.

A police car pulled up and a constable Mark didn't recognise got out. "You requested backup?"

"Yeah, this fellow needs to go to the station. His name is Charlie Gibbon. I've arrested him for criminal damage to the Newsagent's shop."

The constable nodded. "All right, put him in the back and I'll take him to the station."

Mark opened the rear door of the car and Charlie Gibbon climbed inside without protest. The constable went to get back behind the wheel, but Mark said, "You're going to need to contact an Appropriate Adult. He's a vulnerable person."

The constable nodded again. "Okay, no problem. I'll

try to get hold of his parents." He got into the car and drove away.

Mark watched the car disappear and took a deep breath to calm himself. Adrenaline still surged through his veins, making him feel jittery. He realised he was still holding the baton in his hand. He collapsed it and put it away. Less than an hour on the beat and he'd already had to arrest someone. The day had not gone anything like the way he'd expected it to when he'd left the station.

He still needed to get a written statement from Newsagent. He didn't offer a friendly smile to any of the passers-by as he made his way to the shop; he didn't have the energy. The friendly face of policing was going to have to wait until another day.

CHAPTER
TWENTY-SIX

TOM FROWNED at the images on his computer screen. Yorrick had uploaded the twenty-three missing photos from the final roll of film in Edward Barker's camera, and just as the SOCO had said, most of the photos seemed meaningless.

Eleven of the shots showed the boys building what Tom assumed was the hideout mentioned in the Mystery File. These pictures had been taken from a distance, probably with a telephoto lens. Sam and Michael were on Stone Peak, building a frame from tree branches and camouflaging it with pine needles and leaves. Fred the dog was in eight of the photos, running around the hideout and being petted by Sam and Michael, yet the distance from which the photos had been taken suggested the boys were unaware of Edward Barker's presence.

The photographer seemed to have been spying on

the boys, staying hidden some distance away even though his dog had no such reservations.

The other dozen images were puzzling. Barker had taken twelve photos of a clearing in a wood. There was nothing remarkable about it; no obvious reason for the photographer to have taken twelve pictures of such a mundane subject.

"Ryan," Tom called. He needed a second opinion on this.

The DS poked her head through the office door. "You called, guv?"

He gestured at the pictures on the computer screen. "What do you make of these?"

She leaned over the desk, and he caught the scent of her perfume. Floral. Pleasant. Like a meadow on a summer's day. Not that Tom particularly liked meadows, or summer days for that matter, but the scent coming from DS Ryan reminded him of a time when he was younger. A time when he'd been carefree and happy.

Before he'd run away.

That was how Ryan had put it in the pub. It was also how Tom thought of it during his most secret moments.

I ran away to London after my mother died. In the city, amid the hustle and bustle, and the demands of his job, it had been easy to dismiss such thoughts, but now that he was back home, introspection came more easily. This was the first time he'd admitted it to himself, and he had no idea why the scent of Ryan's perfume had prompted such an admittance.

"Barker was definitely spying on Sam and Michael," she said. "Fred is in these photos, but they're all taken from a distance."

"Yes, and what about these?" He pointed at the photos of the woodland clearing.

She squinted at the screen. "I don't know. Maybe he was trying to use the film up, like I did when I was a kid."

"If it was one or two pictures, I'd agree, but twelve?"

"It does seem a bit excessive." Ryan grabbed the mouse and clicked on one of the photos. It filled the screen. Her eyes narrowed as she examined the enlarged image of the seemingly unremarkable patch of land.

"See anything unusual?" Tom asked.

"Nothing at all." She closed the picture and opened others, each showing the same area from a different angle. "This is more than taking snaps to use up the film. Barker has carefully set these shots up so they show the same area from a dozen different vantage points."

"But why? The shots are so tight that there's no way of knowing where this location is. All you can see are trees and the clearing. We need a wide-angle picture to see the surrounding area."

"There isn't one," Ryan said. "All the pictures are close-ups."

Tom sighed with frustration. Perhaps the photos were meaningless after all. Who knew what Baker had been thinking when he'd taken them? The only person who could answer that question was in the mortuary with eleven stab wounds in his body, and he wasn't talking.

Seeming to detect Tom's frustration, Ryan said, "These dozen photos may be worthless, but we know from the others that Edward Barker was following the boys. That's something. It's progress."

Tom didn't share her optimism. Every piece of information they gathered about this case led to a dead end.

"I have a hypothesis," Ryan said.

"All right, let's hear it."

"We know from these photos that Barker was following Sam and Michael. What if he saw what happened to them on Sunday evening and that's why he ended up dead? The killer was making sure he didn't talk."

"But why hadn't he *already* talked? If he knew who killed Sam, why not come to us and report it straight away?"

She gestured at the images on the screen. "Because he didn't want us to find out he'd been following the boys around and secretly taking photos of them."

Tom mulled it over. It made sense. Barker could have been following Sam and Michael on Sunday evening and seen what had happened to them. He might have feared the police finding out about the pictures of the boys, which was why he had hidden them under his bed. But why hide the photos of the clearing as well?

"Something doesn't make sense," he said. "When he gave us those thirteen photos on Wednesday, why didn't he include the pictures of the woodland clearing? Why were they stashed away with the photos of the boys?"

Ryan scrutinised the onscreen images again, clicking the mouse to enlarge a couple of them before shaking her head. "I don't know."

The desk phone rang. Tom picked it up. "DI Brand."

The voice on the other end of the line was male and deep. "Sir, this is Sergeant Johnson at the Chesterfield station. I'm calling because we've got someone in our custody suite you might want to have a word with."

"Oh?" Tom's interest was piqued immediately. "Who's that?"

"Young fellow by the name of Charlie Gibbon. He was arrested earlier today on a criminal damage charge. The shopkeeper whose shop was trashed dropped the charges, but that was after the lad had been fingerprinted. The computer threw up a red flag against his prints. Apparently, they match a set that were found at one of your crime scenes. On a couple of bicycles, I believe."

Tom's grip on the phone receiver tightened. Could this be the break he needed? "Where is Charlie now?"

"In an interview room with his mum and a solicitor."

"I'll be right there." Tom hung up the phone and looked at Ryan. "Charlie Gibbon is in custody. He was arrested on an unrelated charge, but his prints were flagged in the system. They match one of the sets of prints on the bikes."

She raised an eyebrow. "Really? I can't imagine he'd have hurt the boys, guv."

"Whether he did or he didn't remains to be seen. We know for a fact that he touched those bikes after they'd been lying in the mud by the river. He was there, Ryan."

"Want me to come with you?"

He shook his head. "See if you can find someone who might be able to break that code. There must be someone around here with an interest in that kind of thing. Give them a sample to work on, not the entire Mystery File. We want to make sure they're on the level before we entrust them with so much evidence."

"I'm on it, guv." She left the office, leaving behind only the ghost of her perfume.

Tom brought his mind firmly to the task at hand. He would have to tread carefully with Charlie Gibbon. The young man might be willing to talk to the police, but his mother and solicitor would probably advise him not to. They wouldn't want Charlie to implicate himself in the murder of Sam Jones or the disappearance of Michael Roberts.

A sudden thought hit Tom. What if Michael was still alive and Charlie knew where he was?

You're getting ahead of yourself. One step at a time.

Despite the mental warning to himself, he couldn't help but feel that the case was finally opening up. As he left the station and walked to his car, he shook his head, wondering at his own emotions. It wasn't like him to feel this way, especially regarding an ongoing case. He reminded himself that Charlie Gibbon's statement —if there was even going to *be* a statement— might lead to nothing more than another dead end.

Even so, as he started the Saab and drove out of the car park, he felt a sliver of optimism.

CHAPTER
TWENTY-SEVEN

WHEN TOM ENTERED the interview room at Chesterfield Station, after being guided there by the custody suite desk sergeant, he was struck by how large the space was. He'd been in countless such rooms during his career, and they were usually small, pokey affairs that smelled of sweat and stale coffee. A pleasant smell of cherry laced the air in this spacious room, and Tom wondered if it was being pumped in from somewhere or if an air freshener had been used by the cleaning staff this morning and the scent was still lingering.

A digital recorder sat at one end of a wide wooden table. Charlie Gibbon sat at the table, next to a mousey woman Tom assumed was his mother. Next to her, a balding man in a dark blue suit shuffled a sheaf of papers. That would be Charlie's solicitor.

On the opposite side of the table, a young, fair-haired man in a white shirt and light blue tie sat in front of an open folder. The folder was open to a sheet of paper that displayed printouts of ten fingerprints. Charlie's, no doubt.

"DI Brand?" the fair-haired man said, pulling out the chair next to him.

Tom nodded and took the seat.

"For the benefit of the recording, Detective Inspector Tom Brand has entered the room," the man said. He turned to Tom. "DC Fairbanks. I'll be sitting in on the on the interview, since Charlie was fingerprinted here in our custody suite. I've gone over that already for the recording, so anything else —anything involving the Stone Peak case— is all yours. Basically, I'm just here to work the machine."

Tom would have had no problem using the digital recorder —he'd used many in his lifetime, including the older systems that recorded to tape— but he supposed Fairbanks had a right to be here, since it was his station that had discovered a possible link between Charlie and the bicycles.

"Before I hand it over to you," Fairbanks said. "This is Charlie Gibbon, his mother Wendy Gibbon acting as an Appropriate Adult, and Charlie's solicitor Mr Frank Kinsey."

"Good evening, everyone," Tom said, addressing three people on the other side of the table. "As DC Fairbanks said, I'm Detective Inspector Tom Brand. I'm based at the Relby police station and I'm investigating the murder of Sam Jones and the disappearance of Michael Roberts."

Charlie flinched at the words. His mother put a protective arm around his shoulders and whispered a soft "Ssshh" into his ear to comfort him.

The young man's body language resembled that of a frightened mouse cornered by feral cats. Charlie's shoulders were slumped, his eyes locked on the table in front of him. His breathing was so ragged that he shook with every breath. Questioning him was going to require kid gloves, and Tom feared that Kinsey had told Charlie to answer every question with, "No comment." His earlier sense of optimism had all but disappeared.

"Charlie," Tom said quietly, testing the water.

Charlie's body stiffened and he flinched as if expecting a blow. This frightened young man was a world away from the happy-go-lucky Charlie who had visited the newborn kittens in Wesley Brady's barn. That young man had happily chatted with Tom about Sam and Michael. Now, Tom was going to have to work hard to get even a shred of information out of him.

"You remember me telling you I'm a detective?" Tom said.

Charlie nodded, his eyes flickering up to meet Tom's for a brief instant.

Tom leaned forward slightly. At least he wasn't getting a wall of "no comment" answers. "You remember me telling you that I'm a detective?"

Charlie nodded. "Like Sam and Michael."

"That's right, like Sam and Michael. And just like them, I'm trying to solve a mystery. I'm trying to find out exactly what happened to them on Sunday evening. "

"I don't know what happened on Sunday."

"Charlie isn't very good with dates," Wendy Gibbon interjected.

"I see." Tom considered how to rephrase the information. "Do you remember when Sam and Michael's bikes were lying in the mud by the river?"

Charlie frowned for a moment and then nodded slowly.

"That's the time I want to talk about. Do you remember that evening?"

"I don't remember."

"Really? It was only five days ago." Tom stopped himself. He was going down the wrong line of questioning. He took a slow breath and continued. "You remember seeing the bikes lying in the mud, don't you?"

"Yes."

"Do you know how the bikes ended up lying in the mud like that?"

"No. Sam and Michael took good care of their bikes. They wouldn't leave them like that."

"Do you know who *did* leave them there like that?"

"I don't know."

"All right. Why were you on the trail?"

"I have to stay on the trail. I'm not allowed to go near the water."

"Yes, that's a good rule to follow. What I mean is, what were you doing there that evening?"

"Walking. I like to walk there because it's quiet. I need a quiet place."

"Oh? Why's that?"

"My dad shouts at me and when he does, it makes me angry, so I go to a quiet place to calm down."

Tom glanced at Wendy Gibbon. Her eyes now matched her son's, staring down at the table.

"So, your dad had been shouting at you."

"Yes."

"Do you remember what he was shouting at you about?"

Kinsey stepped in. "Is this really relevant, Detective?"

"I don't know yet," Tom said. "It might be."

"He's always shouting." Charlie's voice had risen in both tone and pitch. "He's loud and I don't like it. It hurts my ears, and it makes me mad."

Tom nodded empathetically. "I'm sure it does. So, what was it this time? What made him shout at you?"

"I said I wanted to go and see the kittens and he said, "What kittens?" and I told him they were at Wesley's farm, and he started shouting."

"Your dad doesn't like kittens?"

"He doesn't like Wesley."

"Oh, I see." Tom said, feigning ignorance of the dispute between the two men. "What did your dad say to you?"

"He said, "You stay away from that drunk. He

destroys everyone he comes into contact with." I don't know why he said that. Wesley is really nice."

"Yes, he seemed nice when I met him." Tom's gaze flickered to Wendy again. She was attractive, in a mousey sort of way, but certainly didn't look like the kind of woman who could cause a lifelong feud between two men. Perhaps she'd been different back in the day, when two young men were vying for her affections. Perhaps after twenty-odd years of living with George Gibbon she had been worn her down into the timid creature she was today.

"I like Wesley," Charlie said. "My dad is stupid."

Wendy's eyes went wide with shock. "Charlie, you shouldn't say that!"

"Well, it's true. He's always shouting. All the time. It hurts my head."

"So," Tom said, "you were angry when you went to the river."

"Wait a minute," Kinsey said, leaning forward. "I don't like the way this is going."

"I don't mean he was angry enough to...do anything rash," Tom said. "I'm trying to jog his memory. Take him back there in his mind."

"Oh." The solicitor sat back in his chair. "Proceed."

"You went to the river, and you were angry," Tom said to Charlie. Then he thought of something and backtracked. "Wait a minute. You told your dad you wanted to see the kittens. So why were you down by the river? Why didn't you go to Wesley's house?"

"I went to Wesley's house first. Diane let me see the

kittens. She went with me to see them. But she couldn't stay long because she was cooking. After she went back in the house, I stayed with the kittens for a while and then I went for a walk."

"And that walk took you to the river?"

Charlie nodded.

"For the sake of the recording," DC Fairbanks said, "Charlie Gibbon nodded his head in response to the last question."

"You said Diane went to see the kittens with you," Tom said. "Was Wesley there?'

"No. Diane said he was working in the field."

"Did you see him in the field?"

Charlie thought for a moment, then shook his head.

"Could you say yes or no to the questions, please, Charlie?" Tom said before Fairbanks had a chance to chime in. "Did you see Wesley Brady in the field?"

Charlie shook his head in response, caught himself, and then said, "No."

"Did you see him at all that evening?"

"No."

"Did you see anybody else at all on the way to the river, or while you were at the river?"

"No. It was quiet."

"All right. Tell me about the bikes belonging to Sam and Michael."

Charlie thought for a second. "Sam's bike is old, and it's got a satchel on the back. He said it used to be his dad's bike, but his dad died and went to Heaven, so it's

Sam's now. Michael's bike is newer. I like his best because it looks really cool."

"Right. So how did you find the bikes?"

"They were lying on the trail."

"And there was nobody else around?"

"I already told you I didn't see anybody at the river. I was telling the truth."

"Yes, sorry, Charlie, you did say that. What happened when you saw the bikes?"

I thought Sam and Michael were somewhere around, so I shouted for them. They wouldn't be very happy to know their bikes were in the mud."

"So, you don't think they left them there themselves?"

"No, I already told you that as well. Sam and Michael take good care of their bikes. Somebody else must have put them there."

"Any idea who?"

"Somebody who doesn't like bikes."

"So, you called for Sam and Michael, but they didn't show up." *Because Sam was in the river, caught up among the weeds*, he thought.

Charlie shook his head again, then eyed the recorder and said, "No."

"What happened next, Charlie?"

"I waited and waited, but Michael and Sam didn't come. So I took the bikes." He looked at his mother with worried eyes. "I know I'm not supposed to take things, but I was keeping the bikes safe for my friends. I didn't steal them. I was just keeping them safe."

"It's all right, Charlie." She put a hand on his. "You didn't do anything wrong." She looked pointedly at Tom and said, "Did he, Inspector Brand?"

Removing evidence from a crime scene for starters, Tom thought. There were other offences he could add to that, but nothing would be gained by charging Charlie. "No," he said, "You haven't done anything wrong. Where did you take the bikes?" He already knew the answer to this question, but wanted to make sure Charlie's version of events matched his own understanding. It was possible that Charlie had left the bikes somewhere else, and another person had found them and taken them to the barn. There had been *two* unknown sets of prints, after all.

"I took them to the barn."

"The barn by the river? In the overgrown field?"

"Yes."

"Why did you take them there?"

"I like it there. Dad never goes to the barn."

"I see. You were still avoiding your father. Did you remove anything from the bikes?"

"No, why would I do that?"

"Perhaps you were curious about the mystery the boys were investigating and decided to have a look in Sam's saddlebag." Tom had to make sure that Yorrick's team had possession of everything that had been in that bag. Anything that was missing could contain clues vital to the case.

"No, I didn't do that. The mystery is a secret that only Michael and Sam are allowed to know."

It hadn't escaped Tom's notice that Charlie was still referring to the boys in the present tense. That could be because of the young man's limited understanding of the situation, or it could mean something else. "Charlie, do you know where Michael is?"

Charlie frowned, clearly confused. "Mr Tobin said Michael was missing."

"Who is Mr Tobin?"

"The man at the sweet shop. I went there to buy a Kit Kat, and he said he was sorry to hear that Sam was dead and Michael was missing." His breath hitched and he wiped his eyes with his sleeve. "How can I know where Michael is if he's missing? I need to give him his bike back."

"Don't you worry about that," Wendy said, pulling her son's head to her shoulder and stroking his hair.

Kinsey looked at Tom and said, "Inspector, I think we're done here. Charlie has told you everything he knows."

Tom sighed, his earlier optimism waning with each passing second. The solicitor was right; there was nothing to be gained by questioning Charlie further.

"All right," he said. "I think that's enough for now. If there's anything else, we'll be in touch."

"Can I go home now?" Charlie said, wiping his eyes again.

"DC Fairbanks will make the arrangements for you to go home. Thank you for talking to me, Charlie." Tom got up and left the interview room, turning his phone back on as he walked through the station to the exit. He had three missed calls from DS Ryan. And the phone rang again before he had a chance to ring her.

"Ryan," he said, bringing the phone to his ear as he walked past the custody suite desk. "What is it?"

Her words stopped him dead in his tracks.

"They've found Michael Roberts, guv. The Underwater Recovery Team fished his body out of the river half an hour ago."

CHAPTER
TWENTY-EIGHT

WHEN TOM ARRIVED at the river, the place was awash with the LED glow of hastily erected floodlights. The sky had darkened during his journey here from Chesterfield. The floodlights illuminated the area, but their pale, sickly glow was a poor imitation of daylight. The uniformed officers standing at the cordon of police tape looked washed out and ghost-like; spectres guarding the souls of the dead.

Tom got out of his car and flashed his warrant card at them. They stepped aside and lifted the tape to allow him entry to the place where the Underwater Recovery Team had made their grisly discovery. The long grass on the riverbank *swished* against his trousers as he made his way to a stark white Scenes of Crimes tent that had been set up near the water's edge.

DS Ryan stood outside, her face pale. When she saw Tom, she gave him a weak wave. He went over to her and instinctively placed a hand on her shoulder. "You all right, Ryan?"

"Yes, guv. I just…I was here when they brought the body to the riverbank. It wasn't a pretty sight."

"Get some fresh air. Deep breaths."

The tent flap opened and a Tyvek-suited SOCO poked his head out. "If you want to come in, sir, you'll need to get suited up."

"I'm not coming in. I don't need to see the poor boy. I just need to know what happened to him."

"I'll get Yorrick, sir."

The flap was closed. The air drifting out from within the tent smelled of mud, dirty water, and rotten meat. Tom stepped back. There was no point getting suited up and going in there just to see the state Michael Roberts was in. He'd seen victims who had been spent days in the water before. Michael was in good hands with the Yorrick's team; there was nothing Tom's presence in the tent could do to help the boy. Seeing Michael's dead body certainly wouldn't provide any extra motivation for him to find the killer because by God he already had enough of that.

Someone had killed two twelve-year-old boys in a callous fashion and left their bodies to rot in the river like discarded rubbish. Standing on the bank of that river, in the ghostly glow from the floodlights, Tom silently vowed to do everything in his power to deliver the justice required to avenge the deaths of those poor boys.

Yorrick came out of the tent, tossing his Tyvek suit

into a plastic bag. His face looked even more drawn than usual. He nodded a tired greeting to Tom. "Inspector."

"What can you tell me, Yorrick?"

"At this stage, not much. He's been carried downriver a long way, so his body has collided with rocks, branches, and whatever else is in the river, making it impossible to tell which injuries occurred before death and which were caused afterwards by the environment. The postmortem examination needs to be carried out quickly now the body has been removed from the water, so we should get answers soon. There is one thing, though; his wrists have been bound together behind his back by a length of rope."

Tom felt a chill crawl along his spine like an icy spider. How could someone do this to a child? He couldn't imagine what Michael's final moments of life had been like.

"Sam wasn't tied up," he said, his mind automatically working on the new information and coming up with suppositions. "The killer probably murdered Sam first and had to tie Michael up to make sure he didn't run away while his friend was being drowned in the river." The ice that had travelled the length of his spine now settled in his gut, making him feel nauseous.

"We'll know more when we get the results of the examination," Yorrick said.

Tom nodded, realising he had a grim task ahead of him. "Let me know as soon as you find anything out. I need to tell Claire and John Roberts that their son is dead."

"I'll come with you, guv." The colour had returned to Ryan's cheeks, but her eyes held a haunted look.

"All right." Tom turned away from the tent and made his way through the swishing grass to the car. Ryan walked next to him, saying nothing.

"This isn't how any of us wanted this to go," Tom said, "but at least we've found the boy, and his parents can get some closure."

"I'm not sure they'll see it that way," she said.

"Of course they won't, but it's better than never knowing what happened to their son."

She nodded but her face was unreadable.

As they approached the cordon, it became apparent that the press had caught wind of the heightened police activity and had arrived *en masse* to get a scoop. A dozen news vans sat in the darkness beyond the reach of the floodlights, and reporters and cameramen were poised with their microphones and recording equipment near the police tape, waiting to descend like carrion birds and pick the bones of anyone who might provide them with a story.

As soon as they saw Tom, the feeding frenzy began.

"Inspector Brand, has the body of Michael Roberts been found?"

"What is happening here, Inspector? Why such a large police presence? Is there something the public needs to know?"

"Tell us what's happening."

"Is Michael in the river?"

He told them, "No comment" but some of them followed him to his car, while others followed Ryan, firing similar questions at her.

Tom slid into the Saab and started the engine, gunning it to let the reporters know that he wasn't going to wait around, and they'd best get out of his way. He didn't have time for their games. He had to get to the Roberts house and tell them about Michael before they saw something on the news or read a speculative post on social media.

He drove away from the cordoned area, Ryan's headlights in his rearview mirror. As he reached the main road, her headlights were joined by others as the news vans followed.

"Bloody vultures!" As if he wasn't already angry enough, these idiots who would do anything for a story, invade anyone's privacy, were about to push him over the edge. He called Ryan using the hands-free system in his car.

"They're right behind me, guv," she said as she answered. "What do we do?"

"I'm not leading this pack of vultures to the Roberts house so they can feed off the family's grief. I'm going to the station. Wait for me on Church Street. Park up and turn your lights off."

"Will do."

He ended the call and drove to the station, parking his car in its usual spot behind the building. The news vans idled to a stop outside the front of the building, waiting for him. Some of the reporters got out, microphones in hand, ready to assail him with more inane questions.

Instead of going around to the front entrance, Tom scaled the stone wall that separated the station's car park from the Mermaid's beer garden. As he landed on the other side, he drew the attention of the pub's patrons who were eating and drinking at the outside tables. "Nothing to worry about, folks," he said as he walked past them. "Police business."

He crept around the side of the pub to the front of the building, stealing a glance down the road. The reporters were still waiting for him, van engines switched off. After double checking that their attention was on the station and no one was looking in his direction, he walked briskly across the street and around the church onto Church Street.

Ryan's Jeep was parked halfway down the street, lights off.

Tom made sure he wasn't being followed with a quick glance over his shoulder before climbing into the passenger seat. "Right," he said. "Let's get to the Roberts house."

"How did you manage to avoid them?" she asked as she pulled away from the kerb. "Did you climb over the wall into the pub?"

"That's a trade secret, Ryan. If I let you in on all my methods, you'd know as much as I do, and we can't have that. There's only room for one genius at the station."

She laughed, despite the circumstances. Tom knew that to outsiders —people who didn't do this job— her laughter might seem callous, as might his attempt at humour. But anyone who worked in an environment where death and heartbreak were constant companions —nurses, firefighters, paramedics— would recognise it for what it truly was: a defence mechanism.

There was only so much of the world's cruelty a person could take before needing a suit of armour to protect against it.

By the time they pulled up outside the Roberts residence, all trace of levity had long since disappeared. The atmosphere in the car was sombre.

The lights were on in the house, living room curtains drawn. Tom took a breath before getting out of the Jeep. He was about to destroy any hope the Roberts family had about seeing Michael again.

The night seemed to have become suddenly colder as he got out of the vehicle, but he knew that was probably nothing to do with the environment and more to do with the fact that his body temperature had dropped. It was almost as if he was experiencing the shock he was about to deliver to the Roberts family.

Ryan followed him up the path to the front door, keeping a respectful distance, silent except for the sound of her shoes on the cement path.

Tom took another breath and let it out slowly before knocking on the door decisively. The sounds of movement came from within. Someone approached the door and rattled the safety chain. The door opened and Claire Roberts peered out from the brightly lit hallway.

When she saw Tom, her eyes widened. She stepped back and raised her hands in front of her body as if warding off an attack.

Tom cleared his throat. "Mrs Roberts, can we come in?"

"No." The word came out in a gasp, accompanied by sudden tears. She shook her head. "You can't come in." Her voice was barely more than a whisper as she continued to back into the house. Then she repeated the words but louder this time. "You can't come in; you can't come in." She repeated them over and over, as if they were a mantra that would keep reality at bay.

The sound of movement came from the living room. John Roberts appeared in the hallway, anguish contorting his face when he saw Tom on the doorstep and the state his wife was in. He rushed to her and put his arms around her. She collapsed into them, as if her body had been drained of energy but her tearful eyes remained locked on Tom's. "You can't come in, you can't come in, you can't come in!"

FRIDAY

CHAPTER
TWENTY-NINE

KATE SAT at her desk with a mug of strong coffee and a photocopied page of the Mystery File in front of her. The stick men danced across the page but their various poses, carefully drawn by Sam Jones, meant nothing to her. She had searched for locals who might be able to shed light on the mysterious symbols but had come up empty-handed. The only person who had looked promising —a computer science teacher from the local school— had balked when Kate had sent him a sample of the code.

The coffee was doing nothing to alleviate her tiredness. She'd hardly slept last night, haunted by the image of Michael Roberts' body being dragged out of the river by the Underwater Recovery Team and Claire Roberts' horrified face as she had realised her son was dead.

Aunt Justine and Uncle Gary had found Kate sitting at the kitchen table at 4 a.m. in floods of tears, unable to control her emotions any longer. They had immediately set to work on cheering her up; Gary making light conversation and telling Kate everything was going to be all right while Justine made pancakes which she drenched in maple syrup, insisting Kate needed the extra sugar to keep her energy levels up.

That initial sugar rush had eventually come crashing down like a lead balloon and now she felt terrible, almost as if she had a hangover. Even the sound of Tilly typing was annoyingly loud.

Hazel Owens came into the room. "There's a lady at Reception asking to see DI Brand."

The DI was out, visiting his father at the hospital, then going to Wesley Brady's to verify the story Charlie Gibbon had told him about Sunday evening.

"Did she give you her name?" Kate asked.

"Mrs Janet Davis. She's Edward Barker's sister."

"She probably wants an update on the investigation into his death. Send her in. I'll speak to her." Kate grabbed a spare office chair and pulled it up alongside her desk.

Hazel disappeared through the door and returned with a short, dark-haired woman who looked to be in her mid-forties. She wore a long, white woollen coat despite the warmth of the day and her hair looked freshly cut and blow dried into a short bob that reminded Kate of the hairstyles of the 1920s. She held the handle of a small black handbag in both hands, her fingers and thumbs constantly adjusting their grip as if the woman was nervous.

"Mrs Davis?" Kate said. "I'm Detective Sergeant Kate Ryan. Take a seat."

The woman sat, her body rigid.

"How can I help you?" Kate said.

"I need to talk to you about my brother, Edward Barker," Mrs Davis said. Her accent was southern. If she had grown up around here, she must have moved away many years ago.

"What would you like to talk about specifically? I'm afraid I can't give you too many details regarding the investigation into—"

"No, it's not that exactly. I need to talk to someone about the search that was carried out at his house."

That surprised Kate. Usually when relatives came to talk about their dead loved ones, they wanted to know details of the death, or the victim's last hours. This was the first time Kate had been asked about a property search.

"What do you need to know?" she asked.

"Well, I need *you* to know that Eddy wasn't a drug dealer or anything like that."

"No one is implying he was, Mrs Davis."

"No, they're not, but I've seen the police reality shows on television and I know what happens when large amounts of cash are found during a search. The money is seized because it's assumed to be drug money or something like that. But Eddy wasn't involved in anything like that. So, the money you found in his house can be released from the evidence locker, or wherever you put it."

"Money?" Now Kate was confused. She'd been over the inventory of everything found at Barker's house and there had been no more than a hundred pounds in cash.

The woman nodded. "It isn't in his bank account, so it must have been at the house."

"Mrs Davis, there was only a small amount of cash found during the search. Nowhere near the amount that would be seized as proceeds of crime."

"No, that can't be right. It has to be at the house. There's supposed to be fifty thousand pounds."

"Can I ask why you thought your brother would have that amount of cash?"

"He rang me a couple of days ago and told me he was coming into some money. He owes me and my husband twenty thousand, you see. We loaned it to him when he first started his studio a few years ago, telling him he could pay us back a little bit every month. He rang me on Wednesday and said he would be able to pay back the entire outstanding amount because he was about to receive fifty grand. I've checked his bank account, and it isn't in there, so it must have been at the house."

Kate had no idea where a village photographer would get fifty thousand pounds from in one fell swoop, unless Barker had won the lottery. "I can assure you, Mrs Davis, that there wasn't that amount of cash at the house. Perhaps he hadn't received it yet. He told you he was coming into some money, but not that he already had it."

"But he made it sound imminent."

"Did he say where the money was coming from?"

"I asked him that, and he just said he was getting it from someone who should have covered his tracks better. I thought that was an odd thing to say but he wouldn't tell me any more."

Someone who should have covered his tracks better. It sounded like Barker had something on someone and was blackmailing them. Was that why he was dead? Had this person who should have covered their tracks better decided to do so by killing Barker?

"Mrs Davis, I don't know what to tell you other than there was no more than a hundred pounds at the house. Whatever money your brother was expecting, he obviously hadn't received it yet."

"I see." The woman looked crestfallen. "So, Alan and I are just going to have to kiss that money goodbye, are we? That's the last time I lend anyone anything."

"You'll be able to recoup it and more when you sell Edward's house," Kate suggested, surprised that this woman's only consideration regarding the death of her brother was a debt he owed her from years ago.

Mrs Davis sighed. "Yes, but that will take time. It would have been nice to have the money back now."

Kate had nothing more to say to the woman. It was obvious that Edward Barker was not missed by his family.

"I'll be going then," Mrs Davis said. "I'm being interviewed on television later. I was going to put in a good word for the police investigating my brother's murder, but you've been no help at all." She stalked towards the door.

Tilly spoke up suddenly. "Mrs Davis."

Mrs Davis stopped and turned. "Yes?"

"I was wondering what's going to happen to Fred."

"Fred?"

"Edward's dog. Are you going to take him home with you?"

The woman's nose wrinkled. "Certainly not."

"Oh, so is it all right if I have him? I can give him a good home."

"If you want that mutt, be my guest." She opened the door and was gone.

Kate turned in her chair to face Tilly. "Congratulations on your new dog."

Tilly was beaming. "Thank you. When do you think I'll be able to collect him?"

"Probably today. The vets have finished checking him over and he's fine. I don't see any reason why he can't go home with you straight away."

"Oh my God, I can't wait."

"He'll certainly be better off with you than with Edward's sister."

"Yeah, she's a piece of work, isn't she? You'd never know her brother had just died. I'm going to make a cup of tea; do you want one?"

"I'll have another coffee," Kate said, downing what was left in her mug and holding it out to Tilly.

Coming over to take it from Kate's hand, Tilly

noticed the page of stickmen drawings on her desk. "What's that?"

"It's a code Sam Jones wrote in his notebook. We're trying to crack it."

"You should try Mary Mayweather. She'll work that out in no time."

"Mary Mayweather?" Kate scribbled the name down on her notepad.

"She runs the Castleton Puzzle Club. My mum goes there sometimes. It's mostly just old people getting together to drink tea and eat cakes but Mary, who runs it, is the real deal. She used to be a codebreaker during the war."

Kate felt a sudden surge of hope. A real-life codebreaker. And Castleton was no more than forty minutes from here. "Can you get me Mary's number?"

"Yeah, I'll ring my mum while I make the drinks." She went upstairs to the kitchen and returned ten minutes later with a fresh mug of coffee for Kate and a phone number written on a pink Post-it note. Kate thanked her and dialled the number immediately.

"Castleton Puzzle Club," said a woman's voice as the call was answered.

"Is that Mary Mayweather?"

"No, this is Penny, her daughter."

"Is Mary there?"

"She's out at the moment. Would you like to leave a message?"

"Yes, please. I'm Detective Sergeant Kate Ryan from the Relby police station and we'd like your mother's help with something. We have a code in a notebook that we need to crack."

"A code? Oh, she'll love that. She'll be back in twenty minutes, so I can get her to call you, or you can bring it over for her to have a look at."

"I'll bring it over. Can you give me the address?"

Penny told her the address and Kate wrote it down. "Thanks. I'll be there in about forty minutes."

She quickly drank the coffee, grimacing at the bitter taste, and told Tilly she was going to Castleton and would be back later. As she left the station, she donned her sunglasses against the brightness of the day. Her earlier tiredness was gone, replaced by a sudden clarity and renewed sense of purpose.

It looked like the Mystery File code was finally going to be broken.

CHAPTER
THIRTY

TOM ARRIVED at the Brady farm in foul humour. He'd been driving on the dirt roads and farm tracks for what seemed like hours with no idea where he was going. He had finally arrived at the metal gate with the sign that read *Brady Farm* on the wall next to it purely by chance. The last time he came here, Ryan had been in the passenger seat giving directions. She somehow knew her way around the tangle of narrow roads that all looked exactly the bloody same. He'd needed her this morning; she could have saved him a hell of a lot of frustration.

He climbed out of the car and opened the gate. At least it wasn't muddy. Thanks to the sun beating down relentlessly for the past couple of days, the mud had become hard-packed and dry. The gate swung open with a metallic squeal and Tom drove through before closing the gate behind him.

The one good piece of news he'd received today was

that his father's hip was only bruised and not broken. That meant weeks of rest and rehabilitation rather than months. If all went well and the doctor signed him off today, he could go home tonight. Simple tasks would be a struggle at first, but his dad was used to that because of the arthritis anyway, and Tom would help out as much as he could. That was why he was here in this God-forsaken wilderness in the first place.

A short drive took him to the farmhouse, where he parked and got out of the car. The farmhouse door opened —Tom reckoned it was impossible to approach the house by car and not be noticed— and Diane stepped out. "Inspector," she said, sniffing and rubbing her eyes on the sleeve of her grey turtleneck jumper. "What can I do for you?"

"Are you all right?" he asked as he got closer and noticed her red-rimmed eyes.

"Just allergies," she said, mustering a smile.

It looked like more than just allergies to Tom, but he didn't pursue it any further. "I've been talking to Charlie Gibbon about last Sunday evening," he said. "I'd like to check a few things with you, if that's okay."

"Of course. Come in. I'll put the kettle on." She turned and went into the house, still wiping her eyes.

Tom followed her into the kitchen. One of the kitchen chairs was out of place —Diane had obviously been sitting on it before she'd opened the door— and a scattering of letters and envelopes lay on the table. His inquisitive instincts edged him closer to the table while Diane filled the kettle.

The envelopes all bore the name *Wesley* in a flowery script that seemed to have been made with a fountain pen, but before Tom could see the contents of any of the letters, Diane swooped in and gathered them up.

"I'll just move this mess out of the way so we can sit down," she said, depositing the papers onto the worktop near the kettle and teapot, where she stood over them.

Close at hand, Tom thought. *Where she can make sure I don't read them.* It probably wasn't any of his business but whatever was in those letters seemed to have upset Diane, and his natural curiosity went into overdrive.

She filled the pot and brought it over to the table, leaving it there while she fetched cups and saucers from the kitchen cupboards and sat them on a tray with a milk pitcher and sugar bowl. Placing everything on the table in front of Tom, she took a seat opposite him and said, "Help yourself, Inspector."

He poured a tea for himself, added sugar and milk and tasted it. "Thank you. Now, I'd like to talk to you about last Sunday evening. Charlie said he came over here. Do you remember that?"

"Yes, he wanted to see the kittens."

"Do you know what time it was?"

"I don't remember exactly. It was probably around five, something like that."

"Was Wesley here?"

Her face darkened, almost imperceptibly but it didn't go unnoticed by Tom. "No, Wesley wasn't here."

She was obviously trying to keep her voice steady, but a hint of anger escaped into the tone.

A bit of an overreaction if Wesley was simply working in the field.

"Where was he?" Tom asked lightly.

"I told Charlie he was in the field."

An odd answer. She wasn't saying Wesley *had* been in the field, only that she'd told Charlie he had been.

Tom decided to take a gamble. "Where was he really?"

She hesitated, her eyes dropping to the tea set, unable to meet Tom's gaze. "I'm not sure. I think he was meeting another woman."

The revelation came as a surprise to Tom. It also complicated things. He would need to speak to this mystery woman and verify that she had been with Wesley on Sunday evening. He didn't like loose ends, and the unaccounted whereabouts of Wesley Brady at the time of the boys' murders was very loose indeed. It didn't mean he was a suspect, but Tom would prefer to verify the man's alibi and make sure he *wasn't* a suspect.

"I'm sorry to have to ask, but do you know who this other woman is, Diane?"

She nodded, tears rolling down her cheeks. The crying which Tom had interrupted with his arrival had resumed in full force.

"It's in the letters," she said, waving a hand at the papers on the worktop. "I went up into the attic a week ago to sort out some old clothes for charity and I found them in a shoe box. At first, I thought they were old letters from Catherine, Wesley's wife. I would have been fine with that, but they're not old at all, they're recent. And they're not from Catherine."

She stopped and took a gulp of tea, and angry look burning in her eyes suddenly. "There have been more than a few occasions when he was supposed to be out in the fields, and I went out there to surprise him or bring him lunch and he was nowhere to be seen. I always wondered where he was. Well, now I know. He was in that old barn on George Gibbon's property with his tart."

"The old barn?"

"That's where they met. How disgusting is that?" Her face contorted with revulsion. "That's why I tried to steer you in that direction when you were looking for Michael. I thought that if the police were having a look in there, it might put Wesley off going there. Obviously, that didn't happen."

"Have you told Wesley you know about his affair?"

"No. When I first found the letters, he was in the shed, working on his car. I didn't say anything because I was so shocked. I put the letters back where I found them and stayed quiet. He's gone into town today, so I got them down to have a proper look at them. It's all in there. Her telling him how much she enjoys their secret liaisons and how much better he is than her husband. He's probably written similar letters to her and talked about me the same way." She began to sob, her chest heaving as she threw open a floodgate of emotion.

Tom waited, letting her expel the worst of it.

The sobbing finally subsided to sniffs and tears. "Do you know what the worst thing is? I'm not even sure I'm going to confront him. If we split up, where would I go? My life is here. I love this place. I can't risk losing it all."

"I'm sure you'll come to a decision you can live with," Tom said. "In the meantime, I need to know who the other woman is so I can question her about Sunday evening."

She frowned, confused. "What? Why?"

"I need to account for Wesley's whereabouts."

"I can tell you his whereabouts, Inspector. He was in that bloody barn with his mistress."

He leaned forward and took her hand gently. "Diane, I need a name."

She nodded slowly and sat up straight in the chair as if steeling herself. She cleared her throat and said, "Lois. It's Lois Farrow." Speaking the name brought a new flood of tears.

It was Tom's turn to frown. "Lois Farrow. Are you sure?"

"Yes, she signed the letters. She mentions her husband by name. Henry."

He nodded, his mind racing with a jumble of thoughts. "Have you seen Lois Farrow recently?"

"No, not for a long time. She wouldn't want to show her face around here, would she? She's guilty as sin and she knows it."

"Diane, when was the last time you saw Lois?"

She thought about that for a while. "It must have been the year before last. At the Mermaid, probably. Yes, it was not last summer but the summer before." Her eyes narrowed. "I wonder if that's when she started carrying on with Wesley, because I've not seen her at all since then. Not even in the village. She's obviously avoiding me."

Tom stood up. "I'm going to have to get back to the station. Will you be all right? Is there anything I can get you before I go? Another cup of tea?"

"No, I'm fine. Thank you. I knew I would end up in this state when I got the letters out of the attic. I think I needed a good cry. I'd better put them back up there before Wesley gets home."

"All right. Thanks for your help." He left the house and got into his car, sitting there while he mentally arranged his thoughts into something resembling a logical order.

He recalled the conversation with Henry Farrow and checked his notepad to make sure he wasn't remembering incorrectly. No, everything he remembered about that conversation was correct.

That meant Wesley's movements on Sunday evening were still unknown.

Because wherever he'd been at the time of the boys' murders, Wesley had not been with Lois Farrow. According to her husband, Lois had left over a year ago.

CHAPTER
THIRTY-ONE

KATE LEFT her Jeep in the car park of the Bull's Head pub in the village of Castleton and walked a short distance to the address she'd been given, a stone terraced house whose front door bore a wooden plaque that read *Castleton Puzzle Club*. Kate knocked and waited.

The door was opened by a short, grey-haired woman who peered at Kate through thick-rimmed spectacles. "You must be the policewoman who spoke to my daughter on the phone."

"DS Kate Ryan. I was hoping you could help us with a code we found in a notebook."

"Certainly. Come in." The older woman stepped back, allowing Kate to step into the house.

The living room was furnished in a style that reminded Kate of her long-dead grandmother's home. Three old-fashioned armchairs, complete with crocheted doilies on their arms, were arranged around a small stone fireplace, in which a low fire crackled despite the warmth of the summer's day outside. The room smelled pleasantly of cedarwood and mint.

Framed photographs of what Kate assumed were family members adorned the walls, some colour but most black and white. An upright piano sat in one corner of the room, with more framed photographs — these in small, gilded frames— lined up across its top. In another corner, next to a small window, a bird cage containing a blue and white budgerigar hung from a tall stand. The bird saw Kate and let out a *chirp* that sounded friendly enough.

"Take a seat, dear. Penny is making us some tea," Mary Mayweather said.

Kate sat and a woman in her forties entered the room carrying a wooden tray of tea-making paraphernalia and a large white China pot decorated with a picture of bamboo shoots, birds, and mountains in blue. She set the tray on a small wooden table between the armchairs.

"Would you be a dear and pour for us?" Mary asked her daughter.

Penny got to work and said, "Hi, I'm Penny Mayweather. I spoke to you on the phone."

"Thanks for inviting me over," Kate said. She turned her attention to Mary. "I understand you're something of a whiz when it comes to breaking codes. I heard you were a codebreaker during the Second World War."

Mary smiled warmly. "The Cold War, dear. I'm not quite that old."

"Oh, I'm sorry."

"Nonsense. I probably look old enough to have been in World War 2. Anyway, show me what you've got, and I'll see what I can do."

Kate opened the folder she'd brought with her and handed Mary the photocopied page of stick men.

The old woman's face lit up. "Ah, we have a Sherlock Holmes fan!"

"I'm sorry?" Kate wasn't following.

*"The Adventure of the Dancing Me*n," Mary said, peering over her glasses at the drawings. "From the book *The Return of Sherlock Holmes*, I believe. Holmes encounters a cipher just like this."

"So, it should be easy to solve? I assume the story has the solution?"

"It does," Mary said, nodding, "but whoever wrote this is much too clever to simply copy the code verbatim. It looks like they've transposed the alphabetical correlation of each symbol. It's all been mixed up. Oh, this is exciting!"

"Can you crack it?"

"Yes, I think so. It might take a day or two, but once I work out how each dancing man is connected to the alphabet, it should all fall into place."

"That's just one page," Kate said. "There are more."

"That's not a problem, dear. Once I figure out the key to the cipher, applying the solution to the other pages will be child's play."

"That's great!" Kate was sure this woman would be able to decode the notebook. She obviously knew what she was talking about. "I'll leave you my card so you can contact me when you've figured it out." She took out her business card and placed it on the tray next to the teapot.

Finishing her tea, she said, "I'd best get going and leave you to it."

"Hmm?" Mary looked up from the photocopy. She had produced a pen from somewhere and had already begun to make marks on the paper.

"I'll see you out," Penny said. "Once Mum gets stuck into a new puzzle, she gets completely absorbed."

She led Kate to the door and said, "We'll contact you as soon as Mum's solved it."

"Thanks." Kate walked back to the pub car park. As she was about to get into the Jeep, her phone rang. It was DI Brand.

"Ryan, where are you?"

"Castleton, guv. I think I've found someone who can crack the Mystery File code."

"Good. We need to talk. How about lunch at the Willows?"

"Sounds good to me."

"I'll see you there in an hour." He hung up.

He didn't sound happy. Kate wondered what setback had occurred now. Whatever it was, she was sure they could work through it together. She and Brand made a good team, even if she said so herself.

Five days ago, she wouldn't have expected to be saying this at all. She'd been wary of the DI. Yet here she was looking forward to getting lunch with him and hashing out the details of the case.

She got into the Jeep and set off for the Willows Inn.

CHAPTER
THIRTY-TWO

THE FAMILIAR, comforting smell of wood smoke, beer and food greeted Kate as she entered the Willows Inn. The pub was busy as always and filled with the sounds of chatter and laughter. She'd seen the DI's Saab parked outside so she knew he was in here somewhere. She found him sitting at a table in a corner, some distance away from the bar, beneath a low oak beam. He had printed out one of Barker's photos —one of the mysterious patch of land shots— and was staring at it as he drank a pint of lemonade.

He looked up as she took a seat at the table. "This is the quietest table I could find. Let's get the food ordered and get on with it. What are you having?"

She asked for steak and chips and waited while he went to the bar to order it. He came back with a pint of Coke for her and a wooden spoon with their table number on it. "I'm having cottage pie again," he said as he sat down. "I've missed it since the last time we were here."

"That was only yesterday," she reminded him. He was certainly a food lover, although his trim physique might suggest otherwise. She wondered if he went to the gym.

"Well, that just shows how good it was. Now, let's get to it. I went to see Diane Summers today. She had some letters she'd found in the attic. Love letters to Wesley Brady from another woman. It seems he's been having an affair, meeting his mistress in that old barn, and Diane has no idea where he was on Sunday evening when the boys were being…killed." Despite the fact that their table was some distance away from the rest of the diners in the pub, he lowered his voice when he said that last word.

"He was probably in the barn with his mistress," Ryan suggested.

"Perhaps. The thing is, Diane thinks the mistress is Lois Farrow. She's the one who wrote the letters to Wesley. But he can't have been with her on Sunday evening because Henry Farrow told us Lois left over a year ago."

"Unless Henry Farrow is lying."

"Why would he do that?"

She shrugged, going over the possibilities in her head. "Perhaps he didn't want us to speak to her for some reason."

Brand put his left hand on his chin, his thumb pressing against the corner of his mouth. She'd seen him do this before when he was thinking. After a moment, he nodded. "I wouldn't put it past him. But Diane said the last time she saw Lois was the summer before last."

"So, it sounds like Henry was telling the truth after all and Lois has left," she said. "Wesley must be seeing someone else."

"Since leaving the Brady farm, I've been considering another possibility," he said sombrely. "I want to run it by you."

"All right, go ahead." She could tell from his tone that his thoughts on the matter had gone to a dark place; somewhere only a copper's mind would go.

"I was thinking about Catherine Brady, Wesley's ex-wife," he said. "She and Wesley had a violent past. Then, according to my father, Catherine simply vanished one day. Wesley told everyone she'd done a runner in the middle of the night, but after talking to Diane, I went back to the station and did a quick search on the computer. I can't find any trace of her."

"She could have changed her name."

"It's possible, but based on my admittedly limited search, she doesn't seem to exist."

Kate suddenly knew where he was going with this. "And now Lois is gone as well."

He nodded. "And Wesley Brady has a connection to both women."

The food arrived. They fell silent for a moment while the plates were put in front of them. Kate put salt and vinegar on her chips and waited for them to cool down before eating, her thoughts running over the information Brand had revealed. The topic of Wesley Brady had her thinking about DCI Holt's interest in the man, and her own clandestine investigation into his past.

"There's something I need to tell you," she said. As far as she was concerned, her loyalty was to the DI. Holt's arrangement with her ended here and now. "DCI Holt asked me to report to her directly about Wesley."

"What?" He had a forkful of cottage pie in his hand. He paused before it reached his mouth.

Kate felt a sudden rush of guilt. She hadn't actually reported anything to Holt, but not telling Brand about the DCI's request was a betrayal in itself. "I'm sorry," she said, looking down at her steak. "I should have said something sooner. She wanted me to tell her about what was going on behind the scenes. She mentioned Wesley by name, trying to make it sound casual, but I knew the whole thing was about him."

Brand frowned. Kate couldn't tell if he was hurt or confused. Probably both. She'd gone behind his back and shattered any trust he might have had in her. Her loyalty might lie with him, but she didn't expect that to be reciprocated anymore. She had royally screwed that up.

"I found a connection between the DCI and Wesley," she offered. "When Catherine called the police about Wesley being violent, Holt was the responding officer. She was just a PC back then. She went out to the Brady farm twice."

His forkful of cottage pie resumed its journey to his mouth, and he chewed on it silently. Kate began eating as well, but her food was tasteless. She knew her inner turmoil and disappointment with herself were making it so.

Finally, the DI spoke. His voice didn't betray any emotion. "The DCI probably has her own suspicions about Wesley's involvement in Catherine's disappearance. If she knew the woman back then, she would have taken notice when Catherine suddenly vanished. In fact, I'm surprised she didn't take her suspicions to someone higher up."

"It doesn't look like she did," Kate said.

He went back to thinking, hand on chin again.

"I don't know what she thought she was going to find out," Kate said. "It's not like Wesley was going to confess to us that he killed his wife ten years ago. It isn't even related to the case we're working on."

"Unless it is," he said enigmatically.

"What do you mean, guv?"

He slid the photograph of the woodland clearing across the table towards her. "I've been thinking about these photographs Barker took. To us, they're meaningless. But to someone who knows exactly where the location is, they might mean a lot. A hell of a lot."

She studied the picture. Then realisation struck her out of the blue. "You think this is Catherine Brady's grave, don't you?"

Brand nodded. "I think that's what the boys found. I think that's the Stone Peak Mystery."

She considered the scenario. "Barker was following the boys around, so he would have noticed their interest in the clearing. That's how he would have learned about the grave. I don't know how the boys figured out the significance of the place, but they must have somehow."

"They were watching it from their hideout on the Peak," Brand said. "Maybe they saw Wesley visiting the grave and worked out what it was. Then, on Sunday evening, Wesley sees them and realises they know his secret."

"So, he kills them to keep it quiet." A shudder ran through her. It was unthinkable that two innocent boys had been killed simply because they'd chanced upon a ten-year-old clandestine grave.

"And then he kills Barker when Barker tries to blackmail him," she said.

"Blackmail?" Brand looked surprised.

"Barker's sister came into the station asking if we'd found a large sum of money at Barker's house. Just before he died, he'd told her he was expecting fifty grand."

Brand considered that for a moment before picking up the photo. "So, he must have sent one of these to Wesley demanding money and threatening to go to the police."

"And instead of fifty grand, he got eleven stab wounds."

"As a theory, it makes sense," Brand said, "but we don't have a shred of evidence to support it. We can't charge Wesley with anything yet. We don't even know where this clearing is."

"We need to fingerprint him," Kate said. "See if his prints match the unknown set on the bikes."

"There's no way we can arrest him and print him yet with the little we've got. I'll ask him to come into the station," Brand said, "and interview him under caution."

"We can't fingerprint him in an interview under caution. Not unless he volunteers to let us."

"Perhaps he will. We'll tell him it's for elimination purposes. If those aren't his print on the bikes, he shouldn't have any problem being printed. If he refuses, that act alone will speak volumes."

Kate saw the logic in that. A chat with Wesley might be revealing in a lot of ways. He might even confess and tell them where the grave was if he had a guilty conscience about it. She'd seen stranger things happen during interviews.

"I'll let the DCI know what we plan to do," Brand said, pulling his phone out of his pocket. "Since she seems to have an interest in Wesley, I'm sure she won't object to us interviewing him. I'll find somewhere a bit quieter to talk to her." He left the table and went outside into the car park.

Kate continued to eat. The steak tasted better now that she'd cleared the air with Brand, and they were making progress with the case. She allowed herself to relax for the time since the early hours of Monday morning, when Holt had rung her. She'd been wound up like a tight spring ever since then and now it was time to let some of that tension go. They had a suspect. The evidence, circumstantial though it was, all pointed to him as the killer of Catherine, Edward Barker, and the boys. All they had to do now was build an airtight case against him.

The DI came back inside and took his seat opposite her. His face was like thunder.

"What's wrong?" she asked him.

"I told Holt what we were planning to do, and she said that under no circumstances are we to interview Wesley Brady regarding Catherine. We can talk to him about anything else, but that subject is off limits."

Kate felt the spring tighten again. "I don't understand. Did you tell her about the suspected grave?"

"She was having none of it."

They were back to square one. The DCI had shot them down with one simple phone call. "What do we do now?" Kate said.

Brand considered for a moment. "We still need to know where Wesley was on Sunday evening. We know he wasn't with Lois bloody Farrow. Let's have a word with him when we're done here."

"All right. Maybe we'll learn something useful," she said, with little hope that they actually would.

They finished their meals and went out to the car park. "I'll follow you," Brand said. "I still can't find that bloody farm. I only happened on it by chance this morning."

That raised a smile from her. She got into her Jeep

and waited for Brand to start his Saab and pull up behind her. As they drove out of the car park and onto the road that wound down the hill, Kate wondered what the hell DCI Holt was up to. She wanted information about Wesley, and that seemed to be driven by her connection to Catherine a decade ago. But just when more information might be forthcoming via an interview, she'd taken the subject of Catherine off the table entirely. It didn't make any sense.

"Ours is not to reason why," she told herself. It was a phrase she'd heard since her days as a PC, whenever someone was given an order that seemed illogical. They would shout out, "Ours is not to reason why," and everyone within earshot would join in, "Ours is but to do or die." It came from a poem about the Charge of the Light Brigade by Alfred Lord Tennyson.

Her phone rang. She answered it using the hands-free system in the car. "DS Ryan."

"Hello, dear, it's Mary Mayweather here."

"Mary, hello. I didn't expect to hear from you so soon."

"Well, I've managed to solve the cipher, and I thought I'd best ring you straight away."

"Of course. Thank you. What does it say?"

Mary Mayweather cleared her throat. "It reads as follows. The suspect visited the location in the woods again today. Michael and I followed him there, but we stayed well hidden behind the trees, so he didn't see us. When he got to the clearing, he knelt down on the ground and started crying. Then he got onto his stomach and stayed there for ages, like he was hugging the ground. Michael thought he'd fallen asleep, but I said you can't sleep and cry at the same time. I don't know if that's true. I might have made it up.

"We waited for the suspect to leave the area before we went over there and had a look. Everything looked the same as yesterday. Michael said we were never going to solve the mystery watching the suspect cry and I said we needed to bring spades with us tomorrow and start digging. Michael said where would we get spades from and how could we bring them here on our bikes? I said Well, we've got to do something because there's a dead woman under here and the suspect killed her."

Mary stopped reading. "That's what it says, dear. It sounds like those boys discovered something grisly."

"I need to ask you not to reveal this to anyone else," Kate said.

"Well, my daughter is here."

"Telling Penny is fine. I mean anyone like the press or anyone who might talk to the press."

"I've signed the Official Secrets Act, dear. I won't tell anyone."

"Can I send you the rest of the journal to have a look at?"

"Of course. I look forward to it."

"I'll have someone bring it over to your house later."

"Excellent. I'll get to work on it straight away."

"Thank you, Mary."

Kate hung up and rang Tilly at the station. "Tilly, I

need you to get the rest of the journal pages over to Mary Mayweather."

"Sure thing," Tilly said. "Then I'm going to the vets to pick up Fred. I rang them and they said there's no problem with me collecting him today."

"That's great."

"Oh, yeah, I almost forgot to tell you," Tilly said. "PCs Barnes and Dalton have been called out to a disturbance at the Farrow Farm. That's one of the places you and DI Brand visited, isn't it?"

"A disturbance?"

"A couple of hikers called it in. Some sort of domestic dispute."

"When was this?"

"Just now. Mark and Lily left less than a minute ago."

"I've got to go." Kate hung up and called Brand.

"What's up?" he said as he answered.

She watched him in the rearview mirror as she spoke. "There's been a disturbance at the Farrow Farm. Some hikers called it in. A domestic dispute."

He sighed. "Bloody hell. It's probably Diane Summers. She's probably gone over there to confront Lois. We'd best get over there."

Kate nodded and pressed her foot on the accelerator.

CHAPTER
THIRTY-THREE

TOM AND RYAN arrived at the gate that led to Farrow Farm at the same time as the police car containing the two PCs. The constables — a tall blonde woman and a shorter fair-haired man— looked surprised when they saw their superiors at the location of their call out.

Tom searched his memory for the PCs' names and came up with Mark Barnes and Lily Dalton. They'd both been assigned to the station as village bobbies but, because of the case involving the boys, had been swept up into search parties and allocated more pressing tasks.

"You two come with us," Tom said, opening the gate. He stepped through and set off briskly along the footpath with Ryan, leaving the PCs to close the gate behind them.

"What do you think, guv?" Ryan asked. "Is it Diane come to have it out with Lois?"

"Or there's an argument between Henry and Lois herself," he said. "We were told Lois has been gone for over a year, but I wouldn't discount anything at this point."

As they reached the turn in the path, a woman's voice could be heard shouting in the distance. "Bring her out here, Henry. I know she's in there. I just want to talk to her."

A shouted reply came from Henry Farrow. "Get off my property, you crazy bitch or I'll take my shotgun to you. You're trespassing."

"I need to see Lois!"

"And I told you she isn't here. Now piss off!"

"I'm coming in!" she shouted. Tom now recognised the voice as Diane's. She'd obviously decided to confront Lois after all. She just didn't know that Lois wasn't here. At least Tom *assumed* she wasn't here. After today's events, with the DCI pulling the plug on any investigation into Catherine Brady's disappearance, he didn't know what to believe anymore.

They reached the house. Diane was on the porch, shouting through the closed front door. Henry Farrow was inside, hopefully not holding a shotgun.

"Diane," Tom said as he got closer to the porch. "There's no point shouting for Lois. I don't think she's here. I don't think she's been here for a long time."

Diane turned to face him, her face betraying the confusion she felt. "What are you talking about? She's got to be here. I told you; Wesley was with her last Sunday."

"I don't think he was."

"He had to be. He wasn't on the farm because he was in that bloody barn with *her!*" The thought seemed to inflame the rage within her. She grabbed the kitchen chair that sat on the porch and hurled it through the front window. The glass shattered with a deafening *crash*. From inside, Henry Farrow cried out, "What the hell? Inspector, do something!"

Tom had no choice. Diane might be grieving for her marriage and her life, but he couldn't let her go on like this. She was going to hurt herself, or someone else. He turned to PC Dalton. "Arrest her. Criminal damage."

PC Dalton nodded and stepped forward, taking the handcuffs from her belt. Diane didn't resist. She leaned her forehead against the wall and placed her hands behind her back, waiting for the cuffs. Her rage had burned out and now she seemed resigned to the consequences of her actions. Dalton read Diane the police caution and led her off the porch.

Diane looked at Tom. "I don't know what came over me. I just wanted to ask her why. Why did she destroy my life?"

"She's not here," Tom said. "If you're want someone to blame, maybe you should look a bit closer to home."

Diane said nothing.

"Take her back to the car and get her to the custody suite," Tom told PC Dalton. "I'll see if I can persuade Farrow not to press charges. PC Barnes, go with her."

The two PCs left the clearing and took their charge back along the path.

"Farrow," Tom called. "She's been arrested. It's safe to come out now."

There was no answer.

"Farrow?"

Nothing.

Tom stepped up onto the porch and tried the door. It was locked, of course, otherwise Diane would have been in there in a flash. He went to the broken window and peered inside. What he saw shocked him to the core. He had expected Farrow to be unharmed, since the man had cried out after the window had broken, but it was obvious he'd been hit with flying glass. He sat on the floor, propped up against the fireplace, blood staining his shirt. Pieces of glass had slashed his face. Some of the shards were still embedded in the flesh. Farrow's eyes were wide and staring and he wasn't speaking.

"Ryan, call an ambulance!" Tom gingerly climbed through what was left of the window, careful to avoid the wickedly pointed glass sticking out from the frame. Once inside, he went to Farrow and checked him over. The man was breathing but he seemed to be in shock, and he was losing blood.

Tom examined the wound on Farrow's torso. A piece of glass stuck out of the man's shirt, just below the ribcage. *Best not remove it*, Tom told himself. He looked around for something to staunch the bleeding. Nothing. He quickly moved to the kitchen and found a tea towel. Returning to Farrow, he pressed it against the wound with as much pressure as he could muster.

His patient screamed, eyes darting frantically around the room. At least he was still alive.

Ryan appeared at the window. "Ambulance on its way, guv, but it'll take some time to get here."

"All right. We'll just have to hope he makes it." He left Farrow for a moment to open the front door for Ryan, then went back to pressing on the now-bloody tea towel.

Ryan came in and glanced around the living room. "I don't think Lois is here anymore, guv. There's nothing to suggest more than one person lives here. Farrow was telling the truth about that." She left the room. Tom heard her go upstairs.

When she returned five minutes later, she looked pointedly at Tom.

"What is it?" he asked.

"You should have a look at this picture I found on the bedroom wall, guv."

He gestured to Farrow with his head. "I can't leave Patient Zero here, can I?"

"I took a photo of it," she said, showing him her phone.

The photo showed a framed photo of a much younger and handsome-looking Henry, and a pretty redhead Tom assumed to be Lois sitting at a café table in Spain. They were holding colourful cocktails up to the camera in a "cheers" gesture.

Lois was wearing a low-cut sundress. Hanging around her neck was a gold necklace with a thin and delicate chain. The pendant attached to the chain was shaped like the sun, with wavy rays radiating from the central circle.

CHAPTER
THIRTY-FOUR

KATE PULLED up to the Brady farm gate, followed closely by the DI. The ambulance had taken almost an hour to get to Farrow farm, by which time Henry Farrow had slipped in and out of consciousness a number of times. When he had finally been taken away on a stretcher by the paramedics, Kate had doubted he would survive the journey to the hospital. It would be touch and go at best.

Wesley Brady came storming out of the farmhouse before Kate could get out of the car. He strode towards them with a look of defiance fixed on his face.

"What the hell is going on?" he growled. "Diane rang me to say she's been arrested."

"She's been arrested for criminal damage," Brand said, getting out of his Saab and closing the door. "I was hoping to persuade Henry Farrow not to press charges but he's in no state to make that kind of decision at the moment. Or any decision for that matter."

"Criminal damage? She told me she had an altercation with Farrow, but what's this about criminal damage?"

"She chucked a chair through his window," Kate said.

Wesley threw up his arms in a helpless gesture. "Why would she do that? What's going on? She wouldn't tell me the details."

"Can we come in?" Brand said, nodding towards the farmhouse. "We can have a chat inside."

Wesley looked back at the house, then shook his head. "If you want to have a chat, we can have it here."

"Suit yourself." The DI leaned on the gate. "We want to know where you were last Sunday evening around 5 p.m."

"I was working in the field."

"Is that a euphemism for shagging your mistress?"

Wesley looked taken aback. "I don't know what you're talking about."

"Or were you doing something worse than that?" Brand leaned forward over the gate, eyes locked on Wesley's. "I can't seem to find out exactly where you were. Diane thinks you were in George Gibbon's old barn having it away with Lois Farrow. But we both know that isn't true, don't we? Because Lois isn't around anymore."

Wesley's face crumpled with confusion. "Why would Diane think that?"

"She's seen the letters, Wesley. Love letters from Lois Farrow to you. Diane doesn't know that Lois is gone, so she thinks you were with her on Sunday evening, around the time those two poor boys were being killed by the river."

"Now wait a minute. You aren't going to pin that on me." Wesley backed up towards the house, arms raised as if he could ward off the accusations being hurled at him. "I want a lawyer."

"You don't need a lawyer, Wesley. You just need to tell me where you were on Sunday evening. You weren't with Lois so who *were* you with?"

The farmhouse door opened, and Wendy Gibbon stepped out. Her hair was in disarray, as were her clothes. "He was with me," she said. "Wesley was with me on Sunday evening."

Kate was shocked to see Wendy walking so confidently towards them. Gone was the mousey character with the timid eyes and in her place stood a poised, assured woman.

"Is that true?" Brand directed the question at Wesley.

The farmer nodded sheepishly. "It's true."

"What about Lois?" the DI asked. "The love letters?"

"Wendy and I have only recently rekindled our relationship," Wesley said. "Before that, I was seeing Lois."

"Why did you stop? What happened to her?"

"I don't know. She stopped contacting me the summer before last. I thought she'd had enough of sneaking around behind Henry's back, so I left it at that. Then I heard she'd run off with another man."

"What other man?"

"I haven't got a clue. She never mentioned anyone else to me. It must have been a whirlwind romance."

The DI reached into his jacket pocket and pulled out the photo of the clearing in the woods. He showed it to Wesley. "Do you recognise this place?"

Wesley looked at the picture and shook his head, lips slightly pursed. "No, should I?"

Kate could tell he was being truthful. The picture had no significance to him.

"How about you, Wendy?" Brand showed her the picture. "Recognise it?"

She looked at the picture and narrowed her eyes. "Could be the woods near Henry Farrow's place. I don't know."

Again, Kate had no reason, judging by Wendy's body language, to suspect a lie.

Brand put the picture away. "I've been told not to ask you this question, Wesley, but since this isn't a formal interview, I'm going to ask anyway. What happened to Catherine? To be more exact…is she still alive?"

Wesley shrugged. "I don't know. I was in a bad place back then. A really bad place. Drinking. Fighting. I used to get so drunk I'd wake up in hedgerows, in people's front gardens, and once on the riverbank with my legs in the water. I could have drowned. Catherine left in the middle of the night, and I don't blame her. To be honest, it was a wake up call for me. I cut back on the drinking. Decided to face my responsibilities instead of running away from them."

"And Charlie loves you for it," Wendy said, going to Wesley and stroking his hair. "He might not know you're his dad, but he loves you. You've been more of a father to him than that monster could ever be."

"Oh, I see," Brand said, looking almost at a loss for words. "You're Charlie's father."

Wesley nodded. "Wendy and I got together over twenty years ago and the result is Charlie."

"That's why George has let that field become overgrown and left the barn to fall down," Wendy said. "He suspects that's where Charlie was conceived. He's right, but he can't prove it. So, he ignores it. Just like he's ignored me for our entire marriage."

Kate had been more correct than she'd suspected when she'd told Brand that everyone around here had skeletons in their closet.

"So, you were both in the barn last Sunday around five?" Brand confirmed.

"We were," Wendy said. "I'm just glad we left before Charlie turned up with those bikes. We would have had some explaining to do if he'd caught us in there together."

"Right," Brand said. "I think we've got everything we came here for." He turned to Kate. "We'd best get back to the station."

Kate nodded in agreement. They had a lot to discuss.

CHAPTER
THIRTY-FIVE

WHEN THEY GOT BACK to the station, the place was empty. "Tilly's gone to collect Fred from the vets," Kate said. "She's going to give him a good home."

"I thought she'd end up with that dog. She did seem keen on him." Brand perched on the edge of Kate's desk. "Tell me your thoughts on this." He placed the picture of the woodland clearing in front of her. "I want to see if we're on the same page."

"I don't think that's Catherine Brady's grave and I don't think Wesley killed her. He really didn't recognise the picture of the clearing. It meant nothing to him."

"So what is it?"

"I think it's where Lois Farrow is buried. The story of her running away with another man doesn't ring true. She was having an affair with Wesley. I think Henry found out about it and killed her. I think he's the "suspect" mentioned in the Mystery File. It was Lois' necklace the boys buried on Stone Peak, so they must have got it from the grave. I just hope they didn't go digging to find it." The thought of Sam and Michael digging up Lois Farrow's corpse made her shiver. A dead body that had been in the ground for over a year would give a child nightmares. But then Sam and Michael would never have dreams ever again, good or bad.

"So, we're in agreement," Brand said. "Our suspect is Henry Farrow. The trouble is, we may never find this place." He tapped his finger on the picture of the grave. "And if we don't, I can't see us getting a conviction."

She had to agree. Without a body, Farrow would likely go free. There was nothing concrete to connect him to the murders of Edward Barker or the boys. Sure, his fingerprints would match the ones on the bikes, but he could say he came across them while out on a walk and moved them out of his way. A jury would need more evidence to convict him of murder.

Her phone rang. It was Mary Mayweather's number.

"Mary, I'm going to put you on speaker," Kate said. "I'm here with Detective Inspector Brand."

"Oh," Mary said, "I've seen you on the telly, Inspector!"

"What have you got for us, Mary?" he said.

"Quite a bit actually. I warn you, this isn't pleasant reading."

"I'm sure we can handle it," Kate said.

"All right here goes. There are quite a few entries detailing how the boys followed the suspect to the grave a number of times. But it's this entry which I think you'll find the most useful. It's the final entry in the notebook"

She cleared her throat and began to read. "We visited the grave today and found a necklace hanging from a tree branch. I theorised that the suspect had put it there because it had been special to his wife. We didn't touch it because it's evidence and evidence has to be handled in a certain way. We decided to get something to put it in, so we biked to our houses, and I cut some velvet cloth from my old magic set. Michael stole a Tupperware container from his kitchen. His mum will be mad if she finds out but when we solve the mystery and take our evidence to the police, her Tupperware will be famous!

"We went back to the grave and carefully slid the necklace into the container. We held it by the velvet, so we didn't touch it and contaminate it. Then we had to decide what to do with it. We couldn't take it home in case our parents found it, so we decided the best thing to do was to bury it. We knew the perfect place, high up on the Peak above a spot where we sometimes went fishing. Nobody will ever find it there. And when we're ready, we can take it to the police.

"While we were standing over the grave talking about it, we heard movement. Someone was coming this way. We moved away from the grave as fast as we could and hid behind the trees. Just as we found a hiding place, the suspect appeared. He went straight to the tree branch where the necklace had been hanging and started to shout, "No, no. Where is it?" He started looking on the ground, getting more and more anxious. Then Fred appeared out of nowhere, barking at us. I put my finger to my lips to tell him to be quiet, but he kept barking, and the suspect saw him and then he saw us. We ran. The suspect shouted, "Get back here!" but we kept going.

"We got to our bikes and rode as fast as we could to the fishing spot. We propped our bikes against the trees and scrambled up the Peak as fast as we could, which isn't very fast because it's steep. We buried the necklace and came back down.

"I don't like this game anymore. It's getting too scary. Michael doesn't like it anymore either. Tomorrow, we're going to go to the police with what we know. It's time to go home now. Windmill. Ice. Worms."

"What was that?" Kate said. "Could you repeat the last three words?"

"You heard right," Mary replied. "Windmill. Ice. Worms. Those are the words written using the cipher. It can't be a mistake because they are actual words."

"All right, thanks, Mary." Kate ended the call and quickly scribbled the three words down.

"The boys were rumbled because Barker was hiding nearby," Brand said. "That's probably how Farrow knew who was trying to blackmail him. He recognised Fred. Barker walked the dog along the riverbank every day; it would be easy to find out who he was. What about the gobbledygook at the end of Sam's entry? I find it hard to believe Sam made a mistake with the code."

"He didn't," Kate said, picking up her phone and opening the What3Words app. "I think it's a precise location of the grave."

"What?"

"What3Words is a locator app. You type the words in, and it gives you a location accurate to three metres." She typed Windmill, Ice, and Worms into the search engine and showed Brand the map that appeared on her phone, displaying a pin in the woods near the west side of Stone Peak. "Lois Farrow's grave," she said.

Brand's eyes widened with surprise. "They did it. Sam and Michael actually did it."

SATURDAY

CHAPTER
THIRTY-SIX

AN AMORPHOUS GREY mist hung over the forest floor, twisting through the undergrowth and clinging to fallen trees like spectral fingers. Through this mist trudged a dozen uniformed police officers, eight Scenes of Crimes Officers, and two detectives. They were equipped with digging equipment, police tape, evidence collection bags, and portable ground-penetrating radar.

Kate led the way, using her phone to lead the group closer to the pin on the digital map. It was slow going. The map simply showed the forest as a plain green squares on the map, but the reality of hidden roots, dips in the terrain, and fallen tree trunks made the journey difficult.

Henry Farrow had used a quad bike during his visits, as evidenced by numerous sets of tracks leading from his house into the forest. The SOCOs had placed markers on the tracks for later analysis. They would hopefully be linked to Farrow's quad bike and used as evidence to prove that he had come out here, to his dead wife's secret grave, frequently.

Brand, who was walking next to Kate and trying not to trip on hidden obstacles, wrinkled his nose. "It smells bad in here."

Kate smiled inwardly. This man really did hate nature. "It's moisture in the soil," she said, "and rotting wood and leaves. The canopy is dense here, so sunlight doesn't penetrate to the forest floor. The ground is in eternal shadow."

"Sounds fitting," the DI said grimly.

When at last they arrived at their destination, Kate stopped and held up her hand for the others to follow suit. Before them, the clearing waited. It looked exactly as it had in Barker's photos except for the mist shrouding the ground.

"This is it," Kate said, stepping aside to let the uniforms cordon off the area with tape while the SOCOs donned their Tyvek suits. She and Brand sat together on a mossy stump while the ground-penetrating radar unit, which looked like a small lawnmower, was booted up by its operator and brought into the clearing.

"If you're here, Lois," Kate whispered, "we'll find you."

Two hours later, an area where the GPR had detected disturbed soil had been carefully excavated. The SOCOs, waist-deep in the resulting hole, were now using hand trowels to remove more earth, meticulously examining the contents of each trowel as more dirt was removed from the grave site. Kate knew they were looking for small bones. A body would decompose quickly in the moist soil, and the invasive trowels, even used carefully, could accidentally sever a skeletal fingertip or toe.

One of the SOCOs held up a hand and pointed at the hole in which he and his colleagues were standing. Photographs were taken, the flash illuminating the woodland clearing with stark white explosions that made the trees seem ghostly.

"I think they've found her," Brand said. He moved to the tape and called to the SOCOs. "What's down there?"

"We've got a body wrapped in a blanket, sir," came the reply. "I can see red hair."

Kate felt relief rush into her like a long-held exhaled breath.

Brand nodded. "Good work. Get her out of there." Returning from the cordon, he leaned against the trunk of a large pine tree and looked at Kate. "We've found her, and it's all thanks to Michael and Sam. If not for those boys, she might have remained here for the rest of time."

"The Stone Peak Mystery," she said. "They solved

it." She felt a sudden, shuddering sob rise within her body and she gasped, holding back tears as best she could until they flowed freely down her cheeks. She didn't even know why she was crying, whether it was for the loss of two twelve-year-old boys who had died while playing a deadly detective game, the woman whose body had been wrapped in a blanket and hidden in the clearing, or for her own mother who had also been found dead in the wilderness.

The DI subtly turned his attention back to the clearing and the work going on there. Kate was glad he hadn't tried to console her; she needed to be alone —or at least as alone as she could be out here surrounded by police personnel — and he seemed to recognise that.

By the time Lois Farrow's body —still wrapped in a thin blanket with a faded floral design— was being carefully lifted out of the hole and placed into a body bag, Kate felt utterly exhausted. She also felt as if she had expelled a sliver of darkness that had been growing inside her since this case had started.

SUNDAY

CHAPTER
THIRTY-SEVEN

HENRY FARROW'S room in the Hope Valley Hospital was guarded around the clock by uniformed police officers. Henry had been formally arrested on suspicion of the murder of Lois Farrow, Sam Jones, Michael Roberts, and Edward Barker. He had fallen silent after the charges had been read to him on Saturday afternoon, but on Sunday morning he asked to see detectives Brand and Ryan.

Tom flashed his warrant card at the PC currently stationed outside the hospital room door and entered, closely followed by Ryan. He hadn't mentioned her emotional outburst at the forest clearing yesterday, and he had no intention to. He knew only too well the stress a case like this caused, and how a breakthrough like finding Lois Farrow's body, could bring emotions welling to the surface.

Henry Farrow was in bed, attached to various machines which beeped at various intervals. The man's face was almost entirely bandaged, and Tom guessed the rest of his body, hidden beneath the covers, was too. According to the surgeons, Farrow was lucky to be alive.

"We're here as requested," Tom said. "What do you want?"

"They told me you found Lois." Farrow's voice sounded weak. The confrontational tone he had adopted when they'd first met him was gone, replaced by an attitude of resignation.

Tom nodded. "We found her." He didn't say anything else, didn't mention the blunt force trauma to the back of her skull, or the fact that she had been struck twice with some sort of heavy object. It was murder plain and simple.

"I want to confess," Farrow said.

That took Tom by surprise. The last thing he had expected from the man in the hospital bed was a confession. "Do you want your solicitor present?"

"I don't need some overpaid git in a suit to tell me what to say. I want to make a confession. Do you want to hear it or not?"

Tom looked at Ryan. She raised an eyebrow, every bit as confused as he was by Farrow's sudden attack of conscience.

"I want to hear it," Tom said, "and I want to record it. Is that all right with you?"

"Do what you want."

Tom took out his phone and opened the voice recorder app. He went through the required procedure for a recorded interview, stating the date, time, who was present in the room, and got verbal conformation from Farrow that the man did not want a solicitor.

When the formalities were done, Tom placed the phone on the overbed table and said, "Mr Farrow, tell us how your wife died."

"I didn't mean to kill her," Farrow said. "I mean it wasn't premeditated or whatever you call it. She was out. I thought she'd gone shopping. At least that's what she told me. I was looking for something, I don't remember what, and I found a letter she'd been writing to Wesley Brady. A love letter. It detailed everything she'd been doing with him. In a barn, mind you, like some filthy animal."

He paused in an attempt to control his emotions. "If she'd come back an hour later, I might have calmed down by then, at least enough to have just thrown her out of the house. But she walked through the door just as I was finishing reading the letter. My blood was boiling. I wanted to hurt her as much as she'd hurt me. I grabbed the cast iron door stop and hit her with it. She stumbled backwards into the wall. I hit her again. When she hit the floor, I realised what I'd done. There was blood everywhere. I wanted to call an ambulance, but it was too late."

His eyes were fixed to the ceiling, as if the scene were being projected there. "I didn't mean to kill her," he repeated.

"What happened then?" Tom asked.

"I wrapped her up in her favourite blanket and took her to the forest."

"Where you buried her."

"I buried her in a clearing. Deep and proper, not in some shallow grave where the animals could dig her up."

"When did this occur?"

"Not last summer, but the summer before. I can't remember what day it was. I drank to try and ease the pain. It worked to an extent, but it made my memories blurry."

"Where is the doorstop now?"

"In the house. Behind the door."

Tom couldn't believe his ears. Farrow hadn't even disposed of the murder weapon. He needed to get someone to go out there and collect it as soon as possible.

"Tell me about the boys. Sam Jones and Michael Roberts. Did you kill them?"

Farrow sighed. Tom wondered if it was tinged with regret.

"I had to kill them. They found the grave, didn't they? Followed me out there when I was visiting Lois and put two and two together. They stole her necklace. I thought it might be nice to hang it there for her and those bloody kids stole it."

"What happened by the river on Sunday evening?" Tom asked, steeling himself to hear details about the murder of the two twelve-year-old boys.

"I somehow caught up with them. They were by the

river. They looked tired. I grabbed one of them and tied him up. He fought back, of course, and his mate tried to fight me as well, but I'm not soft. I soon got the little bastard's hands tied behind his back, and then the other one did what I told him."

"Where did you get the rope?"

"Storage box on my quad bike. I always carry rope, things like that."

Tom took a slow breath. "What happened next?"

"I drowned them. First the one who wasn't tied up, then the other one. It wasn't difficult. I just held them under the water until they stopped breathing. Then I took the bikes and threw them in the mud next to the river so it would look like the boys fell in."

Farrow spoke with no emotion as he described his deeds. If Tom had thought he might have even an ounce of regret, he had been sorely mistaken. The man in front of him had a heart as cold as they came.

"Then I had to kill the photographer," Farrow continued. "He sent me a photo of the clearing and a letter demanding fifty grand. Why he thought I had that kind of money, I have no idea." He laughed, then winced as the action made his wounds hurt. "Anyway, he soon learned not to mess with me. It wasn't easy getting into his house. I had to climb over his neighbour's fence to get to his back door. Anyway, I think killing gets easier the more you do it because I had no trouble sending that bastard to Hell. Then I looked around to see if he had any more photos of the grave, but I didn't find any."

He looked at Tom. "I suppose that's it. My confession. Will that do you?"

That will do nicely, Tom thought. There was no doubt about it; Henry Farrow was going to prison for a very long time. The only thing that didn't make sense to Tom was why he had confessed so readily.

"I've got nothing else to live for," Farrow said, as if reading Tom's mind. "I get lonely now Lois has gone."

So, it was nothing to do with the man's guilty conscience or a desire to set the record straight; Farrow had confessed simply because he was lonely and wanted company. Well, he'd have plenty of that in prison, but being a child murderer, it might not be the type of company he was looking for.

"We'll want to talk to you again, get some more details," Tom said, picking up the phone. "But for now, this is enough."

He looked at Ryan. "Come on, let's get out of here."

They went out into the corridor and Tom closed the door behind them. As they walked to the exit, Ryan said, "He was so matter of fact about killing Sam and Michael. I can't believe he could be so callous."

"All that matters is that we've got him," Tom said.

ONE WEEK LATER

CHAPTER
THIRTY-EIGHT

THE FUNERAL of Sam Jones and Michael Roberts was attended by the local community, the police who had worked on the case, and, of course, the media. Tom stood at the back of the church with Ryan during the service and when it was over, went outside with her to face the inevitable barrage of questions from the press.

This time, when microphones were shoved in his face and television cameras were trained on him, he didn't ignore them or mutter a "no comment." He stopped on the church steps, surrounded by reporters from news channels all over the world, and said, "Henry Farrow murdered four people. It is only thanks to Sam Jones and Michael Roberts that justice will be served. It is they who solved the Stone Peak Mystery and it is they who left, not only clues and evidence, but a precise location of the place where Farrow had buried his murdered wife. Sam and Michael are heroes and, as far as I'm concerned, detectives in the truest sense of the word."

He left it at that, striding away to join Ryan as she moved through the graveyard to the gate. "What are you going to do now?" he asked as he caught up with her.

"Go back to my old job, I suppose. Holt doesn't need me here anymore."

"Speak of the devil." He nodded at a black Lexus parked across the road. DCI Holt, wearing a long black coat that matched her long black hair, and the car's bodywork, leaned against it.

"You two did well," she said as they approached her. "Don't think it's gone unnoticed."

"There's just one thing I don't understand, ma'am" Tom said. "Why did you take Catherine Brady's disappearance off the table when we were going to interview Wesley?"

"I didn't want her name bringing up. You thought he'd killed her. I knew he hadn't."

"How can you be so sure?" Ryan asked.

Holt smiled. "Catherine Brady is alive and well and living in Manchester under a new name. I helped her get out of the situation she was in. It was obvious when I attended those domestic abuse calls that she needed help, so I gave it to her. I picked her up in the middle of the night ten years ago and drove her to a new life. I don't want Wesley knowing where she is. Especially since she has a ten-year-old child that he doesn't know about. A man like that destroys everything he touches. He could never be a good father."

"I think you might be surprised," Tom said, looking back at the church where Wesley was talking to Wendy and Charlie Gibbon.

"Leopards never change their spots," Holt said. She looked at them both. "I have a proposal for you. You two work well together. I was thinking of teaming you up. Two detectives are obviously too many for a village police station, but I can widen your jurisdiction to cover more of the Dark Peak area. I've spoken to the DSI, and he likes the idea, especially now you're both darlings of the media. How does that sound?"

"Sounds good to me," Tom said. Ryan was a damn good detective, and he couldn't think of anyone he'd rather work with. He had to endure the countryside a little longer while his dad recovered from his bruised hip anyway, so he might as well make the most of it. And a larger area of jurisdiction suited him down to the ground. At least he wouldn't be bored.

Ryan raised an eyebrow. "I'll need time to think about it."

"Of course," the DCI said. "Take all the time you need."

"I've thought about it," Ryan said after a microsecond. "My answer is yes."

"Good." Holt opened her car door. "Here's to a successful partnership." She got in the car and waved at them through the window before driving away.

Tom looked at Ryan. "First order of business," he said, "is lunch at the Willows."

"You're on," she said. "And you're buying."

"I bought last time."

"You have to buy me lunch to welcome me to my new job."

"Right," he said, rolling his eyes. "Let's go."

"And we need to discuss office arrangements," she said. "I need a more permanent space than the one I've been using. My own office would be nice."

"Don't push it. The best I can offer is steak and chips."

"All right," she smiled. "That will do...for now."

THE END

The series continues in BURY THE MAIDEN. Click HERE to get it!

From the author of The Detective Game
ADAM J. WRIGHT
BURY
THE
MAIDEN
Dark Peak Detectives Book Two

Printed in Great Britain
by Amazon